TRUTH OR DARE

Fast Times at Ridgemont Hall 1

SARA WYLDE

Published in the United States of America by

Sara Wylde

Cover Art by Bad Unicorn

Ebook ISBN 13: 978-1-948001-10-6 ISBN 10: 1-948001-10-1

Print ISBN 13: 978-1-948001-11-3 ISBN 10: 1-978001-11-X

ASHER

"YOU DO REALIZE that staring at me isn't going to cause me to sponta-neously combust, right?" I continued to be very interested in my book on the life cycle of the northern-speckled cicada.

The fact that it wouldn't work didn't stop Huntington Dane III from trying. He continued to stare at me across the table, only now, his irritating mouth was curled into a smirk that had been known to incin-erate panties across campus. Not *my* panties, of course, I couldn't stand the guy. I'd rather fuck a cactus.

More to the point, *he* couldn't stand me either.

"A bloke can hope," he tossed back.

And that accent. It wasn't cute. It was an annoying affectation that he should've lost long ago. He'd been in the U.S. for ten years, and the Bane of My Existence™ for almost as long.

He was still staring.

"Christ, Dane." I growled like a dog and slammed my pen down on the table. "*What?*"

He continued his cool appraisal, gray-blue eyes flickering over me at his leisure. I wanted to squirm but held myself rigid.

"Just wondering," he drawled, "if you're still on about that bloody list."

"What list?" A brick dropped in my gut. I knew very well what list. Very well, indeed. The one titled "Boyfriend Material" he'd stolen from me last week. It was an itemized list of everything I wanted in a man. Dane had already had hours of fun taunting me with the stupid thing. Yeah, that's what I got for trying that "manifest what you want from the universe" crap.

"Don't be coy." His smirk bloomed into a knowing smile that was just as wretched.

"Why do you care?" I didn't like where this was going. If I had more brains than balls, I'd flee to my room and lock the door. Only, I didn't. I sat there, looking at the devil expectantly and waiting to hear what new torture he'd devised for me.

"There are better ways to go about getting what you want."

"At the risk of repeating myself, why do you care?" Dane's interest in anything me-related was suspect and to be treated like a plague.

"It's painful to watch, Cinder Girl. All of this mooning about like an insipid cow because all your friends have things to do on a Friday night and you're at home making your lists and annoying me. Never let it be said I'm not a philanthropist."

I narrowed my eyes. I hated that nickname. He'd been calling me that since Brewer. Since before my father had abandoned us for his mealy-mouthed oatmeal-faced secretary and taken all his money with him. Since he'd become The Bane of My Existence™. It was weird how I hated Dane more than my father, but I did.

I should probably have some therapy. I would, if I could afford it. At the moment, I was barely making ends meet to get my degree. I'd worry about that first. I steeled my spine and sat up straighter under Dane's perusal.

"I don't know what your game is, but—"

He interrupted me. "My game is to get you out of the flat a few nights a week. I don't need you lurking about and ruining the mood."

"I thought you took all of your "shags" to a hotel or something." Yeah, that accent still wasn't cute. Neither was calling women he slept with "shags." He was the grossest human being.

He wrinkled his nose as if he'd just stepped in dog shit. "It's bad enough I have to live in student housing, but you see, I've been cut off for the year. So I'm officially on a...*budget*." He spat the word out like he would a mouthful of raw sewage. They were obviously one and the same in his mind.

I couldn't help it. I laughed with unabashed glee.

"It's not funny." He flashed me a look that would've wounded a lesser mortal.

"Oh, but it is."

He scowled again. "In any case, *my* misfortune has led to an improvement in *your* circumstances."

"How's that?" I had to make an effort not to snort. Undoubtedly, I was pleased by his "misfortune," but beyond that, I didn't see how it applied to me.

"I'm going to show you how to catch and *keep* a bloke with every quality on that list." He said this as if he'd just offered to share some bit of alchemy that could turn shit into gold.

"Who says I want to keep them?" Like I was some virgin of yore looking to reel in a good marriage prospect? I mean, not that I was opposed to marriage. But I had things to do. Like educate myself. Build a portfolio and a nest egg.

"Of course you want to keep him. That's what all you North Bend debutantes want."

"I wasn't a deb," I snarled. "Nor would I be." That was a lie. I would've been, if not for what my father had done. The whole thing was so pathetically cliché. I was lucky to be a legacy and guaranteed my spot at Hollingsworth along with the academic scholarship. Otherwise, I didn't know where I'd be.

The smirk was back at full wattage. "God, Cinder. It's so easy to wind you up. You should work on that." He leaned back in the chair looking very pleased with himself. "You've got to get over your inferiority complex if you ever want to marry money."

"I don't give a shit about money." Which was an utter lie. The only people who could say they didn't give a shit about it were those who had it. Kind of like breathing—you don't really think about it until you can't. Not to say I only wanted to be with someone with money, but I wasn't going to shackle myself to someone with no drive. No ambition. Or no prospects.

"You're such a liar, Asher."

"Pot and kettle, Dane." I pursed my lips.

"I don't lie."

"A lie of omission is still a lie."

"No, the failure of one party to conduct due diligence doesn't constitute a lie on the part of the other party."

I sighed heavily. "Don't you have somewhere to be? Like drowning kittens and swindling old ladies out of their husband's pensions?"

"No more than you have somewhere to be, like mopping the student union to pay for your education."

I was careful to put my pen down oh-so-slowly—carefully. I positioned it just so next to my notebook. To keep from stabbing him in the face. "Maybe working for what you want is a dirty word in your house, but for the rest of the world, it's considered noble."

"So you're a noble savage, then? Is that how you're playing it?"

It would be easier to stomach Huntington Dane if he were stupid, but he wasn't. He had the best education his daddy's money could buy. As evidenced by his reference of the "noble savage" in *The Conquest of Granada*.

Jackass.

I steeled my spine. "I don't have to play anything. I'm myself and you can take it or leave it. I'd rather you left it, and me, alone. What is it you Brits say? Sod off? Is that in a language that you can clearly understand?"

"If you're not playing at anything, why did you make a list?"

"Shut up about the list. It's none of your business." I tried to keep my tone even and unaffected, but I knew I was failing, and miserably.

"It is my business. I live in this flat, too. How am I supposed to get any privacy with you sniffing about?"

"I guess you have to learn how to compromise. You know, like a normal, well-adjusted member of a society that's bigger than your gene pool."

"Why?" He seemed utterly scandalized. "It's stupid to settle for half of what I want when all of it is within reach."

"How's that?" I cocked my head to the side.

"I already told you. I will help you catch any bloke you want with the understanding that you spend most of your time at *his* dorm. It's the least you can do."

"Even if I agree, how are you going to get rid of Conrad and Pandora?" They were the other occupants of the dorm pod.

There were four rooms to each pod that shared a common room and a kitchen. Each room had its own private bathroom and a security lock. It was like an apartment within an apartment.

Too bad I'd gotten stuck with Huntington Dane and his crew of sycophants. Conrad and Pandora were almost as bad as Dane himself. I'd taken to calling them The Terrible Twosome of Gruesome. (Which I haven't trademarked like The Bane of My Existence™. I want everyone to use it.)

"I don't have to get rid of them, love. Unlike you, they have lives."

"Or they just wouldn't want to risk angering you, Prince Smarming."

"There is that." He freely acknowledged it.

For some reason, I thought Hollingsworth would be different than Brewer Prep, but it was just as bad, if not worse than high school. It was the same people, in the same roles, only I couldn't flee home after class because they were there, too.

I could've gone to another school, but Hollingsworth looked so much better on my resume. It would open doors a state college couldn't even see.

"So let's get started, shall we?" He reached across the table and dragged my pen and notebook closer.

"No, Dane. I don't want or need your help." *For this, or anything else.*

"I would say I beg to differ, but I'm a Dane. We don't beg for anything." His superior tone grated on my nerves.

My eyes rolled so hard, I'm surprised they didn't fall right out of my head.

Then he produced that damnable list from his pocket.

My first instinct was to rip it away from him, but he had to be ready for that. So I bit the inside of my cheek and scanned the room for weapons. Too bad there wasn't anything within immediate reach.

"Well, come here, then. I'm not going to bite you." He studied me for a moment. "Of course, if you ask very nicely, I might consider it."

5

He appraised me coolly, presumably looking for some crack in my armor.

I kept looking around for a camera crew. This had to be an episode of some lame prank reality show.

"First on the list." He held up the crinkled paper. "*Funny*." Dane looked back over at me, eyebrow cocked. "Really?"

"Really, what?" I scowled.

"Funny? It's like you copied this list from *Cosmo* or some lame rom-com."

"What's wrong with liking a sense of humor? Should I be looking for dour, repressed and boring?"

"No, but it shouldn't be first on the list. His sense of humor isn't going to be what's getting between your thighs."

"How would you know?" I hated that it came out sounding more like an indignant squawk than a sentence.

"Because I know women." He held up a hand. "And before you argue with me, consider how many sets of thighs I've been between. I know what I'm doing."

"You're not really a repeat visitor, so I don't know that you're qualified to give relationship advice of any kind."

"You just said earlier you didn't want a relationship. What's it to be?"

Damn. He had me there. "Well, the list does say Boyfriend Material. It doesn't say One Off Material, does it?"

His brow furrowed. "Hmm. Perhaps we need another list?" He scrawled something inside my notebook.

"What are you doing?"

"Making a One Off List, what's it look like?" He showed me the book.

"It's surreal we're even having this conversation." I mean, I hadn't thought I'd warranted a trip to the inner circle of hell, yet here I was. I had to acknowledge that Dane might know what he was talking about. With his money, and as much as it killed me to admit it, good looks, he always had his pick of partners.

He put down the pen. "I suppose that it is, but look here, I'm serious about this."

I worried my lip between my teeth. He wasn't going to leave me alone until I agreed. Maybe he could help, but I knew better than to trust Huntington Dane. "Fine. We'll give it a shot, but if you burn me on this, I'll make *Carrie* look like a bedtime story. Do we understand each other?"

He rewarded me with another real smile. Too bad he was such a bastard because that smile was devastating. I bit the inside of my cheek to keep from smiling back. I'd never let myself forget this truce was temporary and even though he had an angel's smile, everything on the inside was all rotten.

"Next items on the list. Smart and witty. Why are those on separate lines?"

"Smart people aren't necessarily witty and those who are witty aren't always very smart."

"And difficult little beast that you are, you must have both?"

"Yes." I lifted my chin in defiance. I kind of liked both defying him and the strange sensation in my stomach when he called me a little beast.

No, you most certainly do not like it. You don't like anything about Huntington Dane. Don't forget: Bane of My Existence™.

"That might prove challenging." He scribbled something on the One Off List.

I perked in my seat like a meerkat watching for predators, trying to see what it was.

"Come here. If you want to see."

"I'm still not sure you're not going to bite. Or pull the chair out from under me before I can sit down." I eyed him.

"I already told you, I only bite on request. Are we doing this or not?"

I noticed he didn't promise anything about the chair, but against my better judgment, I moved into the seat next to him, watching him closely. When my seat didn't explode when I sat down, I leaned over to see what he'd written.

Barclay Scott.

The name was like a junk punch.

I must've have paled because Dane remarked on it. "You look like you're going vomit. Either that's exactly who you want, or so far off base, I may need to rethink my strategy."

My mouth couldn't form words. I hadn't expected him to drive that arrow home with the first shot. I didn't want him to know that I'd dreamed about Barclay Scott for the last three years. His smile. His shoulders. His laugh. His fucking abs, oh my god.

"He fits all of your criteria. Except the witty part. Although, I don't see why he'd feel the need to engage *me* in witty banter."

"You can put him on the boyfriend list." My voice was huskier than I meant it to be.

"What's that? I didn't quite hear you."

"I said, you can put him on the boyfriend list, damn it."

"Ah, so I was right." He looked much too pleased with himself. Dane picked up the pen and made a slash through Barclay's name with a bold stroke and wrote it down on the crinkled boyfriend page. "Any other candidates or is the one?"

I swallowed hard. There was no sneer in his voice, no sign of his usual mockery. What was it he'd said? Why compromise?

"Him. I want Barclay Scott. If you can make that happen for me, I'll stay out of your face until graduation."

"You'd give me four years of peace for *him?*" He snorted. "Love is truly blind."

"I didn't say I loved him. I said I wanted him. And you said you could make it happen. Did you lie?" I needed to turn the attention away from my feelings, or anything else that Dane could use to hurt me in the future.

"No, I can help you get any man you want. Including Barclay Wyndham Scott. In fact, he's having a small gathering tonight at Bear Lake. He has a cabin for the weekend. I, of course, have been invited and may bring a date."

"If I'm going as your date, how is that going to help me?"

"Because Barclay always wants what I have."

Oh, the horror. "Absolutely not."

"Do you want him or not?" His voice slid over me like velvet and lies.

"Yes."

"Then go pack a bag. Assuming you have one."

I didn't. My father had even taken all of our luggage and replacing that hadn't exactly been a priority. My expression must've given me away. I'd have to work on that. He could read me too well.

"Really?" he asked, as if he didn't quite believe me.

"Yeah, really." I lifted my chin again. I refused to let him make me feel ashamed. It was just luggage. I wasn't anything less than he was because I didn't have a bag that had been stamped with someone's name.

"You can use one of mine. Vuitton or Burberry?" He sounded bored.

"Burberry." Well, if he was asking, beggars *could* be choosers and I chose Burberry.

"Good, we'll match. And he'll notice. By the way, don't pack any pretty knickers."

"Excuse me?" Heat infused my face. I didn't want Huntington Dane to know anything about my *knickers*, pretty or otherwise.

"If he sees you there with me, he's going to try to get you alone. It can't be too easy, of course, but he'll manage it. But you can't give in, because he'll 'hit it and quit it' as Barclay is so fond of saying. And if your knickers are ugly, you won't be showing them to him, now will you?"

That feeling was back in my stomach, the sick twisty one, and I knew that there was no way this could end... except badly.

I felt like I was in a movie and we'd hit the point where you're yelling at the heroine, telling her not to go into the woods. But she skips down the path anyway, tra-la-la-ing along, into the deep dark woods where the monster waits.

The heavy feeling in my gut was screaming at me to turn around.

But I kept tra-la-la-ing down path next to Huntington Dane anyway.

STILL ASHER

ON THE DRIVE to Bear Lake, I was still debating all possible outcomes. My brain was fairly spinning, like Clothos weaving the thread of fate.

Okay, so maybe it wasn't *that* serious.

No, I decided, it really was.

I was in a pretty little red Audi convertible speeding toward my destiny with Barclay Scott. Only the devil was at the wheel.

Maybe this wasn't an Audi at all, but a basket and we were headed straight to hell. It *was* going awfully fast.

"You're going to kill us," I said conversationally.

"We'll leave good-looking corpses. Or at least I will." He smirked. "You'll be in your—what is it Pandy calls them? Right. Granny panties."

"I despise you."

"The feeling's mutual, love."

"Stop calling me that," I grumbled.

"Do you like Cinder Girl better?"

"Probably as much as you like Prince Smarming." I crossed my arms over my chest.

"That makes us quite the pair then, doesn't it? Maybe I should be the one on your list. Don't go losing your secondhand clogs at midnight, or I might be forced to do something rash like kiss you."

I gasped. "That's just mean."

"Isn't it, though." It wasn't a question.

I turned to study him as he drove. He wasn't handsome by traditional standards, not like Barclay. His features were too sharp, everything about him was icy and reminded me of winter and the cold. From the blades of his cheekbones to his white-blond hair and his gray-blue eyes that reminded me of antifreeze.

Of course, that's probably what was in his veins instead of blood.

Yet still, there was something about him. Something in the hard line of his jaw, or maybe it was in the width of his shoulders? Perhaps it was the contrast of his hard body, but his skin pale as snow. Somehow, instead of detracting from his appeal, it only added to it. I mean, not for me. But for other women. On other men, it might look sickly and sallow, but it gave him an even harder edge, like a diamond.

"Considering the prospect of a midnight kiss, are you?" He didn't turn to look at me or acknowledge my scrutiny in any other way.

"No. Just wondering why so many women find you attractive."

"I dare you to care." He didn't take his attention off the road.

"What?"

"I-Dare-You-To-Care Syndrome. The less of a fuck I give, the more they want me. It's true for most people. They want what they can't have. You should try it with Barclay."

"Why can't you just be honest? Games are childish." I fiddled with the seatbelt.

"Games are fun, why else would we play them?" he taunted.

"Because you're a sociopath?" I asked in a cheery tone.

He laughed. "You asked why women want me and I gave you the answer. What you do with that knowledge is up to you."

"Only you would find that description of yourself amusing." Of course, I acknowledged that I must have something wrong in my brain to be in my current situation with the aforementioned sociopath.

"I find most everything amusing."

"That's easier than experiencing any real emotion."

"How the fuck would you know what I experience?" His voice was low and gravelly and for first time, I thought one of my barbs might have struck home.

I was torn between filing it away for future ammo and the cold splash of guilt that trickled like ice down my back. He hadn't done anything to me and so far, he hadn't proved this truce to be anything than what it was.

"You're right, I don't. I'm sorry."

The flash of vulnerability was gone and in its place was the Dane I knew.

"Are you trying to kill me? You admitted I was right *and* apologized in the same sentence."

"Is that all it would take?" I snorted. "I've been playing this wrong for years."

He arched a brow.

I coughed. "Yeah, well don't get used to it." I liked things better this way. With him strictly on his side, and me strictly on mine. Lines were drawn and they weren't to be crossed. Seeing him as anything but the manipulative manwhore that he was could only lead to bad things.

"Wouldn't dream of it, Cinder."

"Christ Almighty, my name is Asher. Or even call me by my last name."

"No, I quite like Cinder. The cinder girl who crawled from the ashes and got her prince charming? Why don't you like it?"

"Because it's infuriating." I gritted my teeth.

"Why?"

"Are we playing twenty questions or are you writing a book?" I snapped.

"Writing a book," he agreed amiably, unfazed by my irritation. "Or a list. A *boyfriend* list." He cut his glance toward me with a sly grin.

I eyed him. "Fine. For every question I answer honestly, you have to do the same."

"I have nothing to hide. I'll even let you go first."

Shit. I didn't have any questions in mind because I didn't think he'd agree. So I pounced on our most recent interaction. "Why did you get so angry when I said you didn't feel any real emotions?"

The look on his face made me regret asking. I'd just told myself that we weren't friends and it was good to keep those lines drawn, not to cross them. And what did I do? Launched myself over that line with all the force of a rocket.

"You always go for the throat, don't you?" He kept his eyes focused straight ahead.

If he'd been anyone else, I would've withdrawn the question, apologized for prying. But he was going to make me confess why I hated that he called me Cinder Girl. Fair was fair.

"I like that about you," he continued.

"Wait, now who is trying to kill who? You like something about me? Be still, my exploding heart." I clutched my chest.

"I like plenty of things about you."

"That's not going to get you off the hook from answering my question. Unless you're ready to concede and forego an answer to your own."

"A woman who uses words like concede and forego is going to be bored to tits with a fuckmuppet like Barclay. You could tell him a thesaurus is a newly discovered species of dinosaur and he'd believe you."

"Stop changing the subject, Dane. Answer or concede."

"What do you want me to say? That yes, things hurt me? Yes, I bleed? I do." His voice was strained.

"You'd never let me get away with that answer."

He exhaled heavily and nodded. "From the time I was a child, I've been taught I'm not supposed to feel things and if I do, I should excise it from myself like I would any other cancer. Danes are ruled by logic and cunning, emotion is useless, but it's like a drug and I can't stop it, no matter what I do. So I have to pretend like nothing cuts me. But that's not the hard part. It's the things that actually make me happy I have to hide. Don't enjoy them any more or any less than any other thing. Or it will be taken from me."

I watched his face as he spoke and there was something raw in his expression that confirmed he was being truthful.

That sounded like a miserable way to live. I didn't know what to say to him. He wouldn't want my pity, but I couldn't offer sympathy because I didn't know what it was like to live that way.

I supposed I could identify with hiding what hurt, but hiding my happiness, that seemed like a much worse fate.

"Your turn. Tell me why you hate it when I call you Cinder Girl."

He'd bared himself to me and I'd given him no quarter. I had to expect the same in return.

Why had I started this again? Oh, right. I'd thought he was going to back down.

I summoned my courage. If he could do it, so could I. "Because it's true. My father left us with nothing, and—" I took a breath to keep my voice steady "—I'm just a girl scrounging in the ashes and clawing for more than I've got."

"Well, that escalated quickly."

He seemed as uncomfortable hearing my confession as I was making it.

"So what's our backstory?" I changed the subject.

"For what?"

"Why you're bringing me to the party?"

"I don't need a story. I can bring who I like and my reasons are my own. Remember when I said I don't lie? We don't have to say a damn word. Just act like you belong, and you do, because you're there with me."

It was good to see that things had slipped back into the normal universe and he was once again the same arrogant bastard I loved to hate.

The turn for Bear Lake loomed on the right and I fought the butterflies that slam danced in my stomach. I hadn't been kidding about the Carrie thing. If this was some kind of trick, if I ended up humiliated, I would make him pay.

I didn't know how, exactly, but I would.

"Stop making that face."

"What face?"

"The one where you look like you need some alone time in the loo."

"Alone time? Is there group time?" I held up my hand. "Wait, I don't even want you to answer that."

"You'd know better than I. Don't you birds all flock together?" He cast me a quizzical glance.

"I am not a bird. I'm a woman."

"Whatever."

We pulled up to the cabin and Dane parked behind Barclay's black Escalade. The butterflies were still moshing in my gut, but I tried to tamp them down.

Of course, I failed miserably upon seeing the drop of pizza sauce on my cleavage from lunch. How had I missed this?

"Fuck."

"What?"

I pointed at my chest with both hands.

"Yes, very nice."

"No, not the breasts. What's on them." I pointed again.

He leaned closer and heat suffused my cheeks. The moshing butterflies flapped their wings so fast I wondered if maybe they were hummingbirds. No—bees. Only a thousand bee stings could possibly account for the sensations rushing through me now.

"Is this a trick to get me to put my face in your goods? Because all you have to do is ask."

"No, jackass. Pizza sauce. Right here." I poked myself.

"Oh. I didn't notice it. I doubt Barclay will."

"What about his crew of harpies? They will definitely notice."

"You're not trying to fuck them, are you? What do you care what they think?" He shrugged.

"Dane!" I tried to keep from shrieking, but so far, I'd failed at that, too.

He sighed and his hands went to the hem of his shirt.

I leaped away from him so fast I cracked my head on the window. "Damn it. *Ow.* What are you doing?"

"Giving you another shirt."

"I—have one in my bag."

"One, I'm guessing. Then what are you going to wear tomorrow?"

I bit my lip.

"Here. As I said earlier, I'm a philanthropist. I gave you the shirt off my back. Literally." He smirked.

I looked at the soft, gray shirt in his proffered hand and then back up at his face. Yes, his face. My eyes didn't stray at all to hard ridges of his abs, his defined pecs, or even his broad shoulders. No, not at all.

He narrowed his eyes and jiggled the shirt. "Well?"

"Thank you." I snatched it out of his grasp and eyed him, but he reached in the backseat and pulled another shirt out of a bag. It still had the tag on it. He pulled it over his head and didn't even ruffle his hair.

As if even his hair wouldn't dare to displease him.

"What are you waiting for? An engraved invitation? Let's go."

"Turn around," I mumbled.

"Oh, for fuck's sake."

"Turn. Around."

"I'm not looking, even though it would be fair after the eyeful you got of me."

"You stripped. I can't help it if you put yourself on display."

"To help you."

"Yes, thank you. Turn around." Heat filled me, and I knew my face had to be fire engine red. Which was stupid. Huntington Dane shouldn't make me blush.

"Where do you propose I turn?"

We were still in the car. I hadn't factored that into my reasoning. "Close your eyes."

He closed his eyes and I waved my hand in front of his face to see if I could get a reaction—just to make sure his eyes were really closed.

He grinned.

"You ass."

"Me? You're the one who almost hit me in the nose just to make sure I didn't get a peek at your water bra."

"I am not wearing a water bra."

"No way is all that cleavage you, Cinder Girl. I would've noticed."

"It most definitely is me." I struggled into the shirt.

"Prove it."

"I'm not falling for that."

His eyes popped open just as I pulled the shirt into place. It smelled…good. Not that I expected it to smell like cat litter or anything, but I hadn't expected to like it.

"Falling for what?"

"You know exactly what." I eyed him pointedly before getting out of the car.

He led me up to the door, but rather than knock, he just opened it and walked inside.

The cabin while obviously a rental, was still nice. Probably some-one's vacation home, rented out most of the year to avoid paying taxes. The "rustic" themed décor was decidedly lacking, but I wasn't going to complain.

"Hideous, right?" Dane said aloud.

So maybe I would complain just a little bit. "It's like that buck is looking at me," I agreed and nodded to the deer head on the wall. "All glassy-eyed and *Evil Dead*."

"Can you imagine getting up for a piss and having that thing staring at you?"

I giggled.

"Hey, Hunt. Glad you made it." Barclay said when he caught sight of us in the foyer.

Hunt? I couldn't imagine ever calling the guy next to me anything of the sort. Jackass. Tool. Dane. Never Hunt.

"Cinder Girl here said she wanted to go out. What could I do but oblige?" He shrugged as if he were nothing but a servant to my whims.

I almost snorted.

Barclay turned his attention to me, his blue eyes so clear they reminded me of the waters off Grand Cayman. It was a struggle not to sigh and twirl my hair around my finger.

He was blond too, but not like Dane. Everything about Barclay Scott had this warm golden glow that reminded me of beaches and honey. Not together of course, because that would be messy, but all things good and warm.

"Cinder Girl, huh?" Barclay eyed me.

"Asher." I was proud of myself that I managed to get my own name out in a coherent fashion.

"Barclay Scott." He said this as if I, and the whole Hollingsworth student body didn't know who he was. Of course, I'd been crushing on him since Brewer.

"The intrepid number twenty-four." He was a lineman for the Hollingsworth Grizzlies. "That was a great game Saturday."

"You like football?" he asked, disbelief scrawled on his face.

I decided to be honest. I knew he had tons of women throwing themselves at him. Especially since there was talk he'd be heading to the NFL next year instead of finishing school.

"Not really, although I like football *players*." I didn't care much about the game one way or another but I really liked eye-loving all the man candy. That itself was worth the price of admission.

"Really?" Barclay laughed. "Then what are you doing with Dane?"

"Having the best sex of her life, obviously." Dane didn't even bother to look up from his perusal of the visitor's guidebook that had been left on the foyer table.

I hoped my face wasn't fire engine red. I suddenly couldn't help but wonder what that would entail:

The best sex of my life.

With Huntington Dane.

There was something wrong with me to ever let that thought be birthed into strange and horrible life. I was here talking to Barclay Scott. The Barclay Scott I'd daydreamed about since I first saw him in my Wicked Women of Fiction class. I shouldn't be thinking about Dane at all.

"The best sex of her life. Right now? You're not setting the bar very high. She's not even breathing heavy."

"See? What did I tell you? He wants everything just because I have it," Dane drawled, seemingly bored with the exchange.

Barclay didn't bother to deny it. "The grass is always greener, Hunt."

"I read somewhere that the grass is always greener because it's fertilized with bullshit." I schooled my expression to a mask of innocence.

"Possibly. But I like taking things from Hunt to remind him that even if all of his toys are handed to him on a platter, he should take care with them. Or someone else will."

I got the distinct impression that Barclay was talking about something specific that was just between him and Dane.

"Spare me your sob story, Barclay. You have the same advantages I do."

"Yes, but you grew up with them."

"It's not all it's cracked up to be, mate." Dane put the brochure down and cast a glance over at Barclay. "Where's the wet bar?"

"In the kitchen. Everyone is out back at the bonfire."

"Don't let my brother lead you too far astray," Dane said to me before he strode off toward the wet bar, leaving that bomb in his wake.

MORE ASHER

"*BROTHER?*" I squeaked.

"When it suits him." Barclay rolled his eyes.

I studied him hard, looking for some trace of Dane in his features. Some small clue that they shared any genetic material. I didn't see any.

"So how do you know Hunt?"

I was glad he'd taken the burden of conversation because I had no idea what to say to him, but on the other hand, I didn't want to spill my guts.

"I guess you could say we have a love/hate relationship." I loved to hate him.

"Most people do with my brother. He's complicated." Barclay flashed his thousand watt smile. "Of course it doesn't help that I fuck with him every chance I get."

I saw Dane's game then. This helping me because he wanted me out of the dorm was a win all around for him. He didn't want me and Barclay to actually get together. He had something planned that would make all of this crash and burn at precisely the right moment.

But seeing his game didn't stop me from reaching out for what I wanted with both hands.

I smiled back. "He needs it to keep him humble."

"I take it he gave you the speech about how I'll try to get in your pants—excuse me—*knickers*, just because you're here with him?" He said, his tone light.

"He might have." I nodded.

"Right after I found out that Huntington Dane II was my father, Hunt treated me like his brother. But the first Brewer Prep party I went to I slept with Pandora Heyde. I didn't know they were together."

My eyes widened and I struggled to keep from choking on my own spit. "*Pandora?* You're the reason they broke up?"

"Yeah." He looked like he felt bad about it.

"She's our roommate, you know. Pandora and Conrad. The Terrible Twosome of Gruesome."

"I take it you don't care for Pandy?"

"If she was on fire, I'd spit on her, but only if I had a sinus infection."

"That's pretty severe."

He was laughing, but I realized I sounded catty. So rather than dissecting my childhood misery with my crush, I said, "Rooming with anyone will make you aware of their...*finer* qualities."

"Wait, so you're rooming with Dane, too?"

"Yeah." I didn't offer any further explanation and Dane saved me from further questioning by bringing me a beer.

Relief flooded me. I thought for sure he'd just dumped me in the deep end of the ocean with no life preserver and swam away. I'd never been so glad to see him. Not that I didn't want alone time with Barclay, I did, but I didn't know how long I could keep herself from latching onto him like some kind of fungus.

Definitely not okay.

Barclay's whole demeanor changed when Dane was back in the picture. He was tenser, poised for fight or flight, it seemed. I could definitely understand that. Dane did the same thing to me.

"I didn't know you were living with a goddess, Hunt. I'd have come to see you sooner." He winked at me.

I wondered if he meant what he said about Dane and his toys—if that's how he thought about me.

How they both thought of me.

"He doesn't know he's living with a goddess, either." I took a swig of the beer after I twisted the lid off.

"I would have opened it for you. God, Hunt, you dick. Why didn't you open the lady's bottle?"

"Because it's bad form to give a woman an open drink at a party. Haven't you read the literature?" He said literature like it was three separate words. Lit. Ra. *Chure.*

Barclay was totally unfazed. "You could open it in front of her."

"Asher, are you offended I didn't open the bottle?"

"Not at all." In fact, only yesterday if he'd handed me a beer, I'd wonder if it'd been poisoned.

"There. See? Or is this you taking better care of my toys?" Dane replied tonelessly.

I'd had enough of this toy business. "*Your* toys? Toys run on batteries and don't talk back." I headed out toward the bonfire, beer in hand.

I saw a crowd of people I knew by sight, but hadn't actually spoken to: Sebastian Rathbone, another poor little rich boy manwhore like Dane, Shae Edgecomb, Matt—I couldn't remember his last name, but he played for the Grizzlies, too. A couple of other people milled around, but I didn't know them either.

Shae perked when she saw me. "Thank God, more estrogen."

I laughed. "I'm afraid I brought more testosterone with me, too."

"Oh, is that Huntington Dane?" She tilted her head to the side and peeked around me.

"Yeah."

"Now the game just got interesting," Shae said.

"Why is that?" I asked.

"My friend Jax here has decided to—"

Sebastian interrupted her. "Jesus, not that again. Leave it alone. Why is it so bad she chose me?"

"Because you're a douche?" Matt said, lip curled in a snarl.

"If I'm a douche, what better place for me than between her—"

Matt suddenly stood up and Shae jerked him back down to the ground like an attack dog on a choke chain.

"Really, Bastian?" Shae rolled her eyes.

Sebastian laughed. "Where *is* our fearless Jax, by the way?"

He was a lot like Dane. They could've been separated at birth. I would sooner believe they were brothers than Barclay and Dane.

"I'll go check on her," Matt replied and headed down toward the lake.

"So, where's the rest of the crew?" Shae asked.

"No idea. We're not exactly friends."

Shae's grin widened. "Oh, good. Pandora Heyde is such a crotch cricket."

I would've choked on my beer for sure if I'd been so unfortunate as to take a drink at that moment. "Holy hell, do you come with a warning label?"

"I come with lots of things." Shae smirked.

"Mostly yourself," Sebastian deadpanned.

"And what's wrong with that? At least I know where I've been and I don't have to worry about how I'm getting home in the morning."

I laughed. Shae was just what I needed. "So, what is it that your friend Jax is doing?"

"Getting her V-Card punched. I love her, but she's this total Type A. She has a mission statement and everything."

"I have a list of sorts myself." I sat down next to her.

"Oh, do tell." Sebastian leaned in toward me.

"Not to punch the V-Card, as you put it. Been there, done that. Just what I'm looking for in a man." I brushed it off as if it wasn't a big deal, but hearing Dane read my list aloud made me feel like two kinds of stupid.

Sebastian motioned for me to continue. "And?"

"Does Huntington Dane meet all of your requirements?" Shae asked.

I cocked her head to the side. "Actually, no."

"No?" Sebastian seemed even more intrigued. "This is fascinating. Tell me what's on your list."

"I have to go with no again."

Shae laughed. "This is why you're here with him. He can't fathom a woman who would tell him no. He and Bastian are like two peas in a pretty boy pod."

"I knew you thought I was hot." Sebastian smirked.

"I said *pretty*. You're like a snowflake. Pretty to look at, but you disintegrate on contact with something real."

"If that's what helps you sleep at night, Shae." He stood. "I need another beer. And to make sure Barclay and Hunt haven't killed each other. Or if they're going to, I want to at least capture it for posterity." He waved his cell and set off for the door.

When he was gone, I said, "You and Sebastian?"

"What? No. Oh, hell no." Shae shook her head. "No, way. Jax chose him and I'm not getting anywhere near that."

"If Jax hadn't chosen him?"

"I don't want to think about that."

"Okay."

"You mean, you're not going to pick it to death?" Shae watched me.

"No. You said not to. That generally means, you know, not to."

"Thanks." All the mirth had left her eyes.

I felt bad for her. She so obviously had it for Sebastian, but he was only interested in the temporary and it was obvious that to him that one woman was as good as another.

The fire was starting to die down. "Are you up for some flicks or are you and Hunt headed straight to bed?"

"Uh..." Bed. I hadn't thought about our sleeping arrangements. Oh god, I needed another beer.

Maybe two.

Maybe ten.

No, no. This would be fine. We were roommates, after all, it wasn't like this was anything new. He'd seen me in my onesie bear jammies and I'd seen him—uh, actually I hadn't. He never left his room looking anything less than immaculate, even if it was just to the kitchen. My mind, traitorous bitch she was, flashed back to the car. When he'd taken off his shirt to give it to me.

Why had I thought coming to this was a good idea?

"Hey, Asher," Barclay said as he came through the door. "Wanna go for a beer run?"

Anything to get away from thinking about sleeping arrangements with Dane. "Sure." I popped up. "You want anything?" I asked Shae.

"A pizza. I would cut a bitch for some pizza."

I grinned. "We'll take care of it." Well, I hoped we'd take care of it. I'd just offered to buy pizza with Barclay's money. I turned to look at him for confirmation.

"Jesus, Shae. You eat like a linebacker."

"I'm *hungry*."

Barclay laughed. "Yeah, okay. Don't gnaw your arm off while we're gone."

"I've got something she can gnaw on." Bastian emerged from behind Barclay.

Shae rolled her eyes. "As if I would put that thing anywhere near my mouth. I *know* where it's been."

"You don't even know what I was referring to. Could've been the sucker in my pocket."

"Yeah, there's one born every minute."

"No, really." Bastian produced a cherry tootsie pop from the pocket of his coat.

Shae narrowed her eyes. "Give it."

I watched all of this go down like a tennis match as they lobbed snark back and forth at one another. I knew Shae wouldn't want to hear it, but I didn't even need to meet her friend Jax to know that it was Shae who should be with Bastian.

"I feel like we should just make some popcorn. This is better than anything on Netflix," Barclay said.

"But then there won't be any more beer." I was excited to get some time alone with Barclay away from prying eyes.

Granny panties aside. As much as I hated to admit it, Dane was right about that, it would keep me from flopping on her back like a demented turtle and demanding Barclay take me.

DANE

IF I COULD ADMIT to loving one thing, it would be what's commonly referred to as "stirring the pot."

I love anarchy the same way I love habanero peppers, just enough for a little spice, but not enough to burn it all down.

I feel that way about Asher, too. In small doses, she's just the right amount of fire. But I needed to get her out of the flat. I just needed her to go away.

I had to get my head right.

The last time she'd come out of her room for a late night cup of tea, she'd been wearing this...*contraption*. An adult version of those wee footie jams, but it had a hood. With ears. It was fuzzy all over. It made her look like a pink life-sized teddy bear.

It was ridiculous.

And yet, it had been the most arousing thing I'd ever seen.

The material clung to her arse in the most delectable way. I wasn't sure if I wanted to pet it or smack it. Maybe both. She'd been bent over, rummaging about in the pantry for the sugar, shifting this way and that—like a dance meant to entice me.

But of course, Cinder Girl would never do anything to entice me.

27

In fact, I knew if I'd done any of the things to her I'd been imagining, she'd fall over dead.

Correction—she'd slap the taste out of my mouth, rightly so, and then fall over dead.

It didn't help that I'd started to believe that might just be worth it. One taste of her and it would burn so deep, I'd never need to taste anything else.

Especially when I remembered the way her breasts looked in that thing. The zipper had slid down just above the valley of her breasts. Just enough to show the faint swell of cleavage.

Just enough to make her look so soft, sweet and feminine.

I couldn't get either image out of my head.

No matter how much I wanked. Instead of exorcising the Asher Demon, it had cemented her as my go-to fantasy.

That shite was simply unacceptable. I was a Dane. I couldn't have any weaknesses, and Cinder Girl could be just that because I wanted her. I wanted her more than I'd let myself want anything in a long time.

So I stirred the pot. I threw us all together in this cauldron and stirred things up but good.

Barclay had been wrong when he said that it was Pandy who'd set us at odds. It wasn't. It was Huntington Dane II. Barclay was the bastard, and yet everything he did was gold—I never could measure up. There was always something more my father wanted from me, always some angle I hadn't seen and that wasn't acceptable.

Now I was giving Barclay what I wanted. Wrapped her up like a gift from Barney's. That should exorcise the demon well and proper.

I grit my teeth thinking about them alone together. I rather doubted they'd be back at any reasonable hour. Asher would entice and intrigue him and Barclay would do whatever it took to stake his claim.

I exhaled heavily and pushed the thoughts of them from my mind. This was what I'd come here to do, and I'd done it. When I could separate myself from emotion—from want—there was nothing that could stand in my way. My father was right about that. I knew it was my need to be seen, to be praised, to finally earn my father's approval that kept me from earning those things.

I didn't want to care at all, not because I'd finally get those things I sought, no. Because it wouldn't matter then.

I didn't want it to matter, didn't want it to cut so deeply. Then I'd be free.

I exhaled again and turned my attention to the other partygoers. They needed another splash of spice, another taste of contained chaos. The fastest way to that was a little bit more fermentation.

More beer.

Or at least a pretense of such.

Shae Edgecomb wanted Bastian Rathbone and she would have him tonight. If I had my way. The tension between them was so thick, it was almost a physical entity.

I wondered what would happen to that tension if they hooked up.

"Shae, love, it looks as if you're out." I sat down next to her and handed her a beer.

She narrowed her eyes at me. "You wouldn't be trying to get me drunk, would you?"

"Me?" I gave an exaggerated blink. "Why ever would I do such a thing?"

"Because you're trying to get me naked?"

"True. That, I am." I winked at her.

"You're an ass," she said without any real conviction.

"Am I? I'm not the one lusting after my mate's crush." So, that was a lie. But whatever.

Shae blushed. "I don't know what you're talking about."

"Come now, love. You can hide it from the rest of them, but not from me. We're alike, the two of us."

"I am nothing like you, Hunt."

"Aren't you? Even now you're plotting how to get what you want and as much as you don't want to admit it, part of you doesn't care what about the consequences."

"Oh, and what is it that I want?" She rolled her eyes.

"Bastian."

"I don't." She shook her head, but her pupils had dilated and her posture had gone rigid.

"Please." It was my turn to roll my eyes. "It's so obvious, it's painful to watch. You could have him, you know. Jax doesn't have to know. Bastian would never tell her."

"But you would."

"How am I to know what goes on behind closed doors? Unless you tell me." I gave her a slow, lazy grin.

"Bastian isn't interested in me."

"Isn't he? I think you're the only woman he talks to on a regular basis that he hasn't slept with."

"So, since he *hasn't* fucked me, that means he *wants* to fuck me? Not everyone is as bent as you are, Hunt." Her lips had thinned into a tight expression.

"No, not everyone." He smiled. "Just Sebastian Rathbone." I knew him almost as well as I knew myself.

Shae shook her head slowly. "You're both fucked. I wouldn't do that to Jax."

"Do what to Jax? It's not like she wants to marry him, is it? They're not dating."

"I couldn't." Shae swallowed hard, as if that action could push her back into a safe zone somehow.

But I was determined to pull her out into deeper water.

"Are you trying to convince me, or yourself?" I decided this was the most opportune time to make my exit, and leave her with this bit to chew on.

Now, it was time to find Bastian and see which of his strings I could pull to maneuver him back out to Shae. He was in the kitchen, his hands braced on the island, his head down as if he was trying to center himself.

"What are you doing?"

Bastian looked up, eyes haunted. "Nothing."

"Shouldn't you be doing it outside? Shae looks lonely. Especially since Jax and Matt went down to the lake some time ago."

"She can barely tolerate me." Bastian took another drink of the beer on the counter. "And I can't say I blame her."

"I think she *tolerates* you very well."

His eyes narrowed. "What's that supposed to mean?"

"You and Jax haven't actually made any claims on one another. And who's to know?"

"I'm a bastard, Hunt, but you're diabolical." Bastian sounded almost scandalized.

"Yes, yes I am." I didn't understand why that mattered to Bastian. Then it hit me. I understood very well what Bastian's problem was. He did want to fuck her, but he knew it would be more than a one off. She made him feel. "Get her out of your system."

That's what I was trying to do with Asher, after all. Otherwise, I knew that she'd burn me to ashes. I'd be the one left with cinders instead of the lovely Cinder Girl.

"What's it to you?" Bastian asked, wary.

"I'm bored." I shrugged. Only I wasn't. I was obsessed. I only wished I was bored. Unaffected.

"So you want to light a match and see what happens?" Bastian shook his head. "Or is it because you need to exorcise some demon yourself?"

"I don't have demons." I inspected my fingernails and flicked an imaginary piece of lint from my jeans. "I have opportunities."

Bastian nodded. "I see your game. You brought Asher just to hook her up with Barclay, you want to get Shae in bed with me, but I can't fathom your reasons as to why."

"I already told you. I'm bored."

Bastian crossed around the island and closed the space between us. "How bored are you, Dane?"

I arched a brow. "What do you mean?" I didn't like other people to be in my space like this, but I knew Bastian would see it as some kind of challenge if I gave any hint that it bothered me and I sure as hell wasn't backing down.

"It amuses you so much to turn the gears, why not be part of it, if you're so desperate for entertainment. You want me to fuck Shae, you want Barclay to fuck Asher, who do *you* want to fuck?" Bastian licked his lips. "Or do you just want to watch?"

I hadn't thought it possible, but Bastian leaned in even closer. "Or will you listen, alone in your room—"

"Look, Rathbone. I know you want to fuck me, but I'm not *that* bored." Except, I licked my lips. Only maybe I was, just to prove a point.

"So you've never done it, then? Never shared a woman?" Bastian still didn't back down.

"I don't share anything, Bastian. Not my money or my toys."

"Then you're missing out."

"Perhaps." I nodded. "But even if I were so inclined, I wouldn't share with you."

"Oh?" He didn't sound offended. More curious than anything. "Why's that?"

"It would be too much like fucking myself, and as hot as I am, well, it's been done."

ASHER

I was alone with Barclay Scott.

Something I'd dreamed about.

His truck smelled like pine, aftershave, and new leather. It was intoxicating.

It would probably be bad form to just launch myself onto his lap and kiss him, right?

Right.

I was supposed to be there with Dane. And, granny panties. I had no idea what to do with myself. Especially my hands. Putting them in my lap was weird, but what else was I going to do with them?

I suddenly felt like even my skin was wrong.

"Have you eaten? Do you want some pizza, too?" he asked as he pulled out of the driveway.

"I never say no to pizza."

Shit. That was why I was wearing Dane's shirt at the moment, pizza sauce. Oh god, what if I dropped sauce on this one, too? He'd never let me forget it. Never. I'd be dead in my coffin and at my funeral, he'd stride up to the podium, probably looking distinguished and still hot as hell, (no, Dane's not hot. He's *not*.) and he'd say, "Cinder

Girl, such a tragic loss. Especially since she stained my favorite Brooks Brothers shirt..."

"There's a place down by the resort that has amazing pizza and good imported beer. We could stop there before the liquor store."

It couldn't be this easy.

Was it a test?

"I don't know. We don't want Shae to eat her own foot waiting on her pizza." I wasn't even going to say I didn't think I should be away from Dane that long. Even though I shouldn't. What kind of conquest was I that I'd just drop what I was doing? You had to start as you intended to carry on.

And it wasn't that I wanted to play a bunch of manipulative games. Dane was much better at that than I was, but I also know there are rules to human mating rituals. If Barclay was interested in me only because he thought I was Dane's girl, I had to give us time to get to know each other so he'd have another reason to be interested in me.

Which meant not being too accessible. Or so my mother had always said. Because really, even wearing the granny panties, if he wanted me on my back, I'd probably just fall down like a fainting goat.

"Yes, but we have to eat, too."

"Well, we could get ours to go."

"Or we could enjoy it and get to know each other."

That was what I was after, wasn't it?

"Okay. If you're sure we won't be gone from the party too long."

"No, I won't keep you from Hunt for too long. You'll be back in time for marshmallows and scary stories by the fire."

Yeah, that was the scariest story I'd ever heard.

"Good. So the rumor on campus is you're going to the NFL next year."

"I still haven't decided, actually."

Then he was quiet, so I pushed a little more. The silence in the truck was deafening. It was weird that it seemed he didn't want to talk about himself. "But you have an offer on the table?"

"I do."

"That's really great." I leaned back in the plush leather. It was his turn to carry the conversation and so far, nothing was happening.

"What, you're not going to quiz me about which team, how much the offer is, if I have an agent..."

Then I realized the problem. "No. That's none of my business and if you wanted to talk about it, I assume you would."

"Interesting. So you don't have an opinion about it?"

"I do. But again, we don't know each other well enough."

"If we did. What would you say?"

So he didn't want to talk about it until I didn't talk about it and then... Oh my god. If the ground underneath the truck could just open a massive cosmic sinkhole and swallow me, it would be great. "Uh..." I laughed.

"No, I really want to know. Let's call it testing the waters."

Why was everything a test with these people? And then I remembered how I used to be one of them. How exhausting to live that way.

"Okay, whatever it is, I think you should take it, but I think you should still go to school. You can go online. Still get your degree."

"Why?" His body language had changed. Whereas before, talking about this had seemed to make him close up, he was now angled toward me and open. He actually wanted to hear what I had to say.

"Football is a very physical sport. You have to do something when your career is over. You could have a long career, or an injury could take out both your knees on your second season. Education is never a waste."

"That's what I was thinking. I considered declining the offer and finishing school first. Coach said I was crazy."

"I don't think that's crazy at all. I think it's smart to think about the long-term prospect of anything that you do."

"Including dating?" He studied me.

"Yeah, definitely including dating."

"So are you and Hunt that serious?"

"Oh, hell no." I tried not to cough. "This is just for fun. But you never know."

"So you don't date poor?"

"I wouldn't say that. I *didn't* say that. Technically, I'm poor." For some reason, it wasn't as hard to say to Barclay as it was to Dane. Even though it wasn't really an admission. Everyone knew what John Warren had done to his family.

"That doesn't mean you'll date poor."

"I don't date..." I looked for the right word. "Prospectless, if that makes sense. I don't care if the person I'm with has money. I care that they have drive and ambition."

"To get money."

"To survive. To take hold of life by balls and own it. Not to be a passive victim. And why not to have money? I've had it. I've lived without it. I'd rather cry in a Mercedes than a Pinto."

"Too true."

"Good. I thought you might think I was some kind of gold digger. I've got as much ambition for myself as I do for anyone I might consider for a long-term relationship."

"Hunt isn't in your long term?"

He was testing me again. "Isn't that what I said? We're just having fun, and he is a lot of fun."

"Just checking." He smiled at me. "You should let me know when you're done having fun with Hunt."

"Oh, should I? Why would I do that?"

"So you could have fun with me." He pulled to a stop in front of another log cabin styled building with a neon sign in the window that read, "open."

"Hmm. I don't know, Barclay. You want to have fun with me, but only because I'm having fun with your brother. I think that's the fun part for you." And that was a big turn off for me.

He got out of the truck and opened my door. "That definitely has its appeal, but I like you, Asher."

Warmth bloomed in my stomach and spread through my limbs.

I didn't say anything, because as nice as it was to hear that he liked me, he didn't know I was on the same planet he was until today. Not really.

It was Dane that made him take notice of me.

But it wasn't Dane who was here getting pizza and beer. He was back at the cabin, probably trolling for his next "shag."

I wondered who it would be. If he'd have the decency to at least wait until we weren't playing at... whatever we were playing at.

I sounded stupid even in my own head. I needed to get a grip on myself. Remember the mission. Stay objective. Get what I wanted. It shouldn't be that hard.

Barclay held the door for me and we went inside and sat down in a red leather booth. The tables were covered in red gingham table cloths and each table had a small candle flickering at the center.

It was warm, inviting, and cute.

But the menu was actually a dream come true. This was gourmet pizza. You could have anything from roasted garlic cloves to non-dairy cheese substitute, and cauliflower crust. I was impressed.

He was right. The beer list was incredible.

It didn't matter that we weren't twenty-one. These places around the resorts didn't card when the name would be as recognizable as Barclay Scott's. The same when we went to the liquor store to buy the beer.

"See? I didn't lie."

"Is that remarkable?" Shit. Why did I say that? Why was I always such a... me.

But he laughed. "No. Like Hunt, I think the truth is its own best weapon."

"Why does it have to be a weapon?"

"It doesn't." He looked at me for what seemed like forever before speaking again. "You're different from all the other women Hunt usually pursues. I think he may actually really care about you."

I couldn't help it. I choked. Yeah, that would be a cold day in the innermost circle of Hell. I took a drink of my water and chose to ignore the last part of his statement. No one needed to be thinking about that. It was a stray maggot that had crawled up out of... I couldn't think of anywhere worse than Hell. Except a world where Huntington Dane and I had any gentle feelings for each other.

"Why do you think that's a compliment?"

"Most women like to think they're 'different.' That they'll be The One."

"That's all misogynist bullshit." And depending on Barclay's reaction to what I'd just said, he might not be the guy for me after all.

"Huh. Really? Why?"

"Why? Because that implies that all the other women he's been with are somehow less. That we all only want one thing. That it's a big competition. It's not."

"But they were less. They weren't honest like you are."

"Maybe you just weren't listening."

"Maybe I wasn't. I'll do better."

I was completely surprised by his response. "Interesting."

"Good. We've established that we're both interesting and *interested*." He winked at me.

"Maybe, but I'm not done with Dane just yet."

"Why do you call him Dane?"

"It was something we started when we were young. He's always called me Cinder Girl and I've always called him Dane."

"So you went to Brewer?"

"I did. You don't remember me?" I pretended to be offended, but I laughed.

"I think I'd have remembered you."

"Obviously not."

"You were right. I wasn't paying attention."

I laughed again. "So you're pretty good at this banter thing. What are your other talents?"

He raised a brow. "You mean besides the obvious?"

"If you're referring to sex, I think that's subjective, don't you?"

"No. I have a gift."

I snorted. "You all think so."

"We do. But why not pride myself on being a good lover? You can't be good at it unless you put your partner first. Whatever it takes to get her there first, I'm game."

"Oh, for a second I thought you were going to tell me you had a magic penis."

He looked confused. "You mean I don't?" But he laughed.

I was having fun with him, but he was trying so hard to get into my pants, that I didn't need the granny panties.

An hour ago, if he'd said, "Asher, bedroom, now," I'd have trotted right over and presented myself for his pleasure, and mine.

Now? After talking to him? I wasn't so sure.

I could hear Dane in my ear saying, "I told you so."

"I'm going to say something else that's probably going to piss you off."

The server came with our pizza. "The others will be waiting for you at the counter when you're ready for your check. Can I get you guys anything else?"

Barclay looked at me and I shook my head. She went back through a pair of swinging doors to the kitchen.

"That was nice of you to pick up pizza for everyone."

He looked at me expectantly. "So take a bite first."

"You want me high on cheese before you drop this bomb on me?"

"Exactly."

I took a bite and I had to admit, it was really good pizza. The cheese blend was unlike any other.

"You really aren't like other women. At least, any of the other women I've been interested in. And before you argue with me, or tell me I'm being a sexist jerk, I can feel myself losing ground here. I like you. I want you to like me. But all the things that have always worked aren't working here."

"Be yourself. Let me get to know you."

"Like you know Hunt?"

It occurred to me that I did know him pretty well. As well as anyone could, probably. That's not to say I knew his darkest secrets. He hid those from everyone, including himself. "Yeah. I've known him a long time. We haven't always been friends, but I know who he is."

"Are you sure about that? He calls you Cinder Girl, like Cinderella. Who is he in that equation? Prince Charming? Because I have to tell you..."

"I don't need you to tell me who your brother is. I don't need a knight on a white horse."

"What do you need?"

"Someone real."

"I'm not made out of plastic, you know."

He was only pursuing me so intently because of Dane. "Neither am I."

"Hey, I'm sorry."

"For what?"

"This went from fun to that-escalated-quickly. I try to play the game with Hunt, not because I like it, but to survive. It's not like walking on eggshells with him, but on landmines."

I could imagine growing up with him would be hell. It was for me and I wasn't even related to him.

"Dane doesn't have to have anything to do with our friendship."

"Doesn't he? You're with him."

"It's a temporary notion. We all know that. Just let things run their course."

"I guess I can try to do that. But you know my brother. He could manipulate the course of a river if he really wanted to."

"He could, but all rivers eventually lead to the ocean, one way or another."

"So are you guys staying for tomorrow, too?"

"We are." I had no idea if we were, but I wanted to.

I realized something that I already knew logically, but I hadn't internalized. Barclay Scott wasn't a fantasy. He was a real person, with real feelings, real flaws, and real pain.

While he had all the qualities I'd checked off a list, he was more than that.

How had I let myself forget that?

Barclay and I both had ulterior motives for wanting the other person. I should want him for himself, too. Not just because he ticked off a bunch of boxes on a list.

I could also admit I'd been on edge, too. Part of me didn't believe he could want me for me, so I was looking for all the reasons why he wouldn't.

Maybe I wasn't actually ready for a relationship.

"Hey, you know what? Maybe we were both trying too hard."

"You?" he snorted.

I decided if I wanted honesty from him, I had to be honest too. "I had a crush on you back at Brewer."

Well, there was honest and there was throwing myself under the bus. If I could put it in the past, it was honest, but it couldn't hurt me now.

"Really? I was just Hunt's bastard brother then."

"You were nice. You helped me pick up my books when Pandora knocked them out of my hands."

"I don't remember that."

"Right. I wouldn't expect you to. Because it wasn't special. You would've helped anyone. That's what I liked about you."

He looked down, and for a moment, it seemed like he was embarrassed. "I'm not that kid anymore, but I'm wishing I was."

"And I'm not the girl who would let Pandora knock my books out of my hands anymore. So, how about we start fresh? I'm Asher Warren. Yes, my father is *that* John Warren. I'm majoring in business and finance. I'm a dog person. I like long walks on the beach, midnight conversations, and 90's alternative."

He laughed. "Okay. I'm Barclay Scott. Yes, my brother is Huntington Dane. I'm majoring in sports medicine, I'm a dog and cat person. I like working out, rock climbing, midnight conversations, and all music except hick-hop."

"What's hick-hop?"

"It's country that's trying to be hip-hop. I'm down with country. I'm down with hip-hop, but not together."

"That sounds horrible. I think we're united on that front."

"Oh good. If you said you loved hick-hop, I'd have to leave you here."

"Fair enough."

I realized I'd scarfed down three pieces of pizza, and managed not to get any on Dane's shirt. Things were looking up.

"You ready for the liquor store?" He grabbed the check. "Your non-white steed awaits."

DANE

I DIDN'T LIKE IT, of course, when I saw them return and Cinder Girl was all smiles.

God, I'm an arsehole. I was so jealous I couldn't see straight. I wanted her to smile like that with me.

Only with me.

She must've noticed my scowl. "What's wrong," she mouthed.

I schooled my features and I reminded myself this was why she was dangerous. She made me forget all of my hard-won lessons. Just seeing her peeled away my mask and I had to work to get it back into place.

I gave her a slow, lazy smile and mouthed, "Not a thing."

I could tell by her expression she didn't believe me, but that didn't matter. I sauntered over to them.

"Did you have a nice time on your playdate, darling?"

Her smile was nothing short of radiant. It almost knocked me flat. I'd never seen it before. It was blinding. It was beautiful.

And I was smug. She didn't smile like that at him.

Mine.

No, not yours, you stupid git. That was the point of this, wasn't it?

"I did. I had pizza and we brought back enough beer to last

43

through at least tomorrow. We are staying tomorrow, aren't we? *Darling?*"

For a second, I thought she'd channeled Pandora. But Pandora would never eat pizza. Not where anyone could see her anyway.

"Whatever Cinder Girl wants, Cinder Girl shall have."

She leaned in so close to me, I thought she was going to kiss me. And she did. On the cheek. The touch of her lips on my skin was too much, and not enough.

"Thank you."

Oh, she wasn't getting away with that.

I put my arm around her waist and pulled her close. Asher was pliant and soft. Touching her was everything I imagined it could be. I couldn't be the only one feeling this, and if I was, it would be official. This was hell.

Of course, it would be more of a hellscape if she felt it, too. Because there was no way anything real could ever happen between us. I couldn't afford to be weak.

And Asher, she wouldn't let me be anything but. I know feelings aren't weakness for everyone, but they are for me.

I leaned close to her ear. "You're a quick study, but if you think you're going to outplay me, think again."

She looked up at me, brown eyes wide and guileless. "I wouldn't dream of it. I was just trying to thank you."

"Thank me later." And before I could think better of it, my lips crashed into hers, but I retreated before she had time to react. To anyone watching, it would seem like a casual brush of lips, but it was anything but. It was guerilla kissing. It was warfare.

When I pulled back, she wore a look of what seemed to be utter devastation. Which was what I'd intended, wasn't it?

She touched her fingers to her parted lips and I didn't know if she was checking for wounds, or to make sure it had really happened. If I was being honest with myself, I wanted to do the same thing. I was sure her lips were made of sugar and razorblades.

It was my fault. I'd done this.

I'd been so afraid to lose, I'd crossed a line that even I knew better than to cross.

"At least I didn't get pizza sauce on your shirt," she said, her voice monotone.

"Should I thank you, then? The same way you thanked me?" I still hadn't let go of her. The curve where her hip met her waist was still under my palm and I wanted to follow it both up and down. I wanted to touch her everywhere.

I thought I'd dealt the devastating blow. But I couldn't have been more wrong. She looked up at me again with those guileless eyes. "I don't know." She swallowed hard. "Do you want to?"

My cock was already hard, but somehow, it was harder. The idea of kissing her, really kissing her had found purchase in the rotten soil of my imagination. Sure, I'd thought about it before, but she was offering this to me.

This was here.

This was now.

This was real.

"Yes," I confessed. "Which is why I won't. I think we both know better."

She exhaled a breath it seemed she'd been holding and the spell was broken. "Good. Don't do that shit again. That's crossing the streams in such a way, I wouldn't be surprised if it summoned a demon or something."

"You're right about that."

Except it had summoned a demon. One of lust and want and desire. If it was just lust for her body, that would be one thing. I could seduce her, she'd shown me she wasn't immune. But the desire was for more than just her screaming in tongues beneath me. It was for *her*.

How awful. Horror of horrors, to be sure.

And goddamnit, she'd gotten the last word. She was the one who crossed the line and kissed my cheek.

To be fair, we hadn't outlined the rules. So she wasn't technically breaking them. I couldn't be angry with her for that. Only myself.

Of course, rules were made to be...

Stop.

"So is tonight scary story night?" Barclay asked with an easy grin. "Or is it Truth or Dare?"

I rolled my eyes. I pretended to hate those kissing games, but really, I loved them. It was a prime chance to do my favorite thing and stir the pot. Which was why everyone said they hated to play with me.

But they loved it.

Drama always went down.

"Scary stories. Definitely. In fact, I dare you to scare me," Asher said. But then she turned to me. "Not you. You're terrifying."

I couldn't help it. I laughed.

"I don't think you're supposed to say that about your boyfriend," Barclay said.

Shae came in and snatched a whole pizza. "I don't know. I think it's healthy. Any man I date better live in utter fear of my displeasure."

"Of course you would say that," Bastian added, grabbing his own pizza. "I think it's cool to be that naked with someone they know what terrifies you. It's brave. Good on you, Asher. I don't know that I'd choose someone as diabolical as Hunt, but you're packing in the lady balls department. I'll give you that."

Part of me admitted that she was terrifying too, but I wasn't going to tell them that.

"We terrified each other enough earlier, I think." That was as close to an admission as I was going to get. Ever.

To my surprise, Asher leaned into me for a moment before pulling away.

"All right. Asher has spoken. It's scary stories. You want to get everyone out by the fire? It's almost dark. I'll get the marshmallows," Barclay said.

As the sun went down, so did the temperature. Even though we were next to the fire, Asher was shivering.

I knew better.

I did.

But she and Barclay kept exchanging these secret looks. Although that was why I'd brought her here, it couldn't be too easy. I was helping Asher, really, by staking my claim.

I touched her arm. "Shall I get you a blanket?"

She smiled again. "That would be nice. Thanks."

"They're in the hall closet," Barclay said.

A few other guys got up and followed me. I chose a large plush one that would cover us both and headed back to the fire.

I wrapped it around my shoulders and held one arm like a raised wing. "Come here."

Her lips pressed together in a tight line, but then she saw that's what other couples were doing too.

Even Barclay, with a girl named Lauren.

And Bastian and Shae. "This is just for warmth, right?" Shae said, as she trundled under the blanket with him.

"Yeah," he said. "Just for warmth."

Jax and Matt were still nowhere to be seen.

She scooted into me, her back against my chest and I wrapped the blanket around her. Asher stopped shivering, but shortly after, she started squirming, trying to get comfortable.

Which played hell on my hard cock. All that friction. She had to be able to feel it against her arse. She had to.

"Be. Still." I hissed in her ear.

"I can't. I don't know what to do with my hands and something in your pocket is poking me," she hissed back.

I sighed. "Put your hands wherever you like, love."

"You're not cute."

"And that's not something in my pocket."

She stilled.

"Really?" she squeaked.

"So you think what happened earlier only happened to you? I thought I was clear."

She coughed. "You were, I mean, but I didn't believe you."

"Are you two quite finished?" Shae glowered. "I'm trying to tell the story of the dark, dark woods and the dark, dark house."

"Sorry." Asher coughed. "Carry on."

I suddenly didn't know what to do with my hands either. I mean, I knew what I *wanted* to do with them. There was a fine line between carrying on the charade and shooting myself in the knob.

Asher made the choice for me. She settled my arms around her waist and her hands on top of mine. It was intimate, but it was also the safest thing for both of us. I leaned back against the log behind me and we finally eased into a position that was as comfortable as either of us were going to get.

She smelled like vanilla and pizza. I found it strangely arousing. Just like everything else about her.

I was fine until I realized my thumb was grazing the edge of her breast. Then, that was all I could think about. I wasn't aware of anything else around us. Not the story Shae was telling, not the hookups that were happening as people wandered off from the fire out into the surrounding woods or back into the cabin. Not even the chill bite to the air.

Just Asher, and each place where our bodies made contact.

Nothing had ever felt this good.

I tried to move my hand, but it startled her and she jerked, somehow shoving the fullness of her breast right into my palm.

We both froze.

I wasn't good at apologizing, but I hadn't meant to grope her. I tried to find the right words. Of course, that would be easier if I let go of her breast. I didn't want to alert everyone who was left around the fire what was going on beneath our blanket, either. Although, surely, much more was happening between Lauren and Barclay.

She made no secret of squirming to get closer to him, and the shit-eating grin on Barclay's face was a pretty obvious tell.

Asher took my other hand and guided it to her breast. Her nipples were hot points against my palms and when she exhaled, her breath was shaky. When I pressed my lips to her throat, in a strangely chaste kiss, I could feel the pulse of her heart.

I didn't know if she wanted to piss Barclay off, or if this was really what she wanted from me, but I couldn't let that matter. I shouldn't be here.

But I couldn't stop.

Not now that she'd put my hands exactly where I'd wanted them to be.

I moved my hands over her oh-so-slowly, taking my time. Paying attention to when her breath caught in her throat, when she swallowed a gasp, and when she arched in for more.

She was so responsive, it would be easy to figure out which of her buttons she liked pushed.

My hands were under her shirt now, beneath the cups of her bra, strumming her hot little nipples. All the while, Shae finished her story.

When she was done, we were the only ones left.

And we didn't notice when Shae left, either.

Asher had closed her eyes, and her little claws were digging into my thighs. I wanted to make her come. I wanted to see her face while she did. I dipped my fingers ever lower down her stomach and made long, lazy circles over her skin.

I was fast approaching another of those lines that shouldn't ever be crossed.

But I wanted it.

And so did she.

She leaned her head back against my shoulder. "Hunt," she whispered.

That's when I knew I had to stop. She'd called me Hunt instead of Dane. The line was perilously close. She'd already crossed it.

"Everyone's gone inside. Or to the woods to fuck."

"Uh-huh." She turned her face into my neck and pressed her lips there.

It was an invitation. One I wanted nothing more than to accept.

"Even Barclay. He's not watching anymore."

"I don't care."

A coldness washed over me. I dug it up from the darkest part of my guts. I needed some armor. "Did you forget who you were with, Cinder? That we're here to get rid of you?"

She froze.

"I guess I did. But you can't blame me, can you? I guess you really do live up to all the hype." She pulled away from me. "You're a good enough fuck that it's easy to forget what a vile person you are."

"Told you." The cold chill permeated my bones and I welcomed it.

"You did. But you can't blame me for not believing you."

I followed her into the room with our luggage and looked at the bed.

"I don't suppose you'd be a gentleman and sleep on the floor?"

"Not a chance. But *obviously* you, and your footie jams, are safe from me."

"It's not that I'm worried about being safe. I don't want to touch you."

"No chance of that either, is there?" I pulled off my shirt and she turned away.

"You could at least change in the bathroom."

"Why? I sleep naked."

"Of course you do." She wriggled and squirmed until she pulled her bra out of the sleeve of her shirt.

My shirt, against her bare skin.

"You didn't bring your footie jams?"

"No." She crawled into the bed, rolled over to face the wall, the covers up to her chin.

The cold chill retreated long enough to make me feel like a bastard, but better this now, than later when it could be catastrophic for both of us.

I dug the soft loungers out of my bag and changed into them before crawling into the King-sized bed.

She was so close, but so far away.

"You still want Barclay?"

"I don't know."

"Make up your mind. Let's not waste each other's time."

"I'll let you know when I've decided. I won't be pushed into anything just because you need a place to get your dick wet in peace."

"Fair enough."

I lay there in the dark for a long time staring up at the nothing on the ceiling trying not to replay the soft touch of her lips on my neck. Or the invitation to take everything I wanted.

And the pain I'd caused us both by denying this thing between us.

ASHER

I woke up shivering.

Even though I was cocooned in the giant, plush comforter, leaving Dane with only the sheet, I was still an icicle.

How could I have been so stupid?

From now until the day I died, I'd remember last night by the fire and how I'd forgotten not only who I was, but who he was. I'd be ashamed of it until I died. I'd be eighty years old and I'd wake myself up in the middle of night and my face would burn remembering what I'd done. Long after he'd forgotten it. Hopefully.

For a moment, I'd let myself pretend it was okay to take him and his actions at face value. I'd let myself forget we were enemies.

No, I hadn't just let myself forget.

It had been washed away by the fire that bloomed volcanic between us.

I was ashamed to admit my body was still on fire. Jesus Fucking Christ, when his hands had been on my breasts, I'd wanted nothing more than to turn around and climb on top of him and give him the ride of our lives.

At first, it was because of the sensation his touch wrought in me.

Now, lying here in the dark next to him, even after how he treated me, I still wanted it. And part of it was because of who he was.

It gave me a sick little thrill to think Huntington Dane had a hard-on for me. I wanted to fuck him because I knew he hated the idea. It was the ultimate weapon to stab him where it hurt.

What was actually wrong with me?

It was like Dane was some kind of infection and I'd caught that fever. I just had to ride it out. *Ride. It. Out.* God, I couldn't think about that.

I'd focus on trying to get warm in a non-friction type of way. If I didn't freeze to death first.

I stifled a snicker. It would be fitting I'd freeze solid in bed with Dane. After all, he had ice in his veins.

"For fuck's sake, Cinder Girl. You're shaking the entire bed," he drawled. "Are you cold or crying?"

"As if I'd ever let you make me cry." But I had teared up. His words had cut me deeper than I wanted to admit.

"If I get up and turn on the fireplace, will you be still?"

"Maybe," I mumbled.

The mattress moved when he shifted and he got up and went to the wall. It was a gas fireplace. Not my favorite, but I guessed it would have to do.

Soon, a fire crackled in the grate sending a warm light spilling into the room.

And damn him, he'd never looked as utterly hot as he did in that moment. His hair was slightly mussed, and I'd never seen it less than absolutely perfect. I could feel an obsession blooming at the way that errant lock curled over his forehead, and his pajama pants looked so soft. Yet they rode low on his hips and...

... I couldn't help it.

My eyes were drawn down to his cock.

He was hard.

Or a monster.

Maybe both.

I looked away and rolled back over away from him.

"Do you think that now there's a fire, you could share the blanket?"

"No. You're used to the cold. It's in your veins."

"It has to be."

"No, it doesn't." I pulled the blanket tighter. "And I'm still cold."

"Of course you are. You're the sort who has to stand right in the fire to stay warm." He said it like it was an accusation.

"What's wrong with that?" I tried to keep my voice steady, but I failed.

"Nothing, but it's not how I'm wired. Do you understand?"

Was he... apologizing? No, no. Don't start deconstructing him. I'd learned long ago that when people show you who they are, you have to believe them. Making excuses for what they did, trying to paint their shit up like a flower in your head only led to more pain.

"I understand well enough."

"If you did, you wouldn't still sound like a kicked puppy, Asher."

"Sorry about that. I'll be back to the bitch you love to hate tomorrow." I gave him some of the blanket.

"Do you promise?" he said, his voice soft.

"You're not playing fair, Dane. And I know that's not new for you, but here, right now, can't you just be decent?"

"I can't say I like it, but I'm trying. That's what you don't understand."

"You're right. I don't understand. You push me away and then you pull me back, and I want to think you're just being your usual shitty self, but I don't think you are. But then, I decide I'm probably like all the other women you've discarded. Making excuses in my own head to explain why you do what you do, except there is no excuse."

"There's really not. And if you just accept there's nothing more to me than the Dane you love to hate, we'll be fine. We have to go back to the way things were. This new state of things is untenable."

"What if..." I licked my lips. "...what if we gave in to this? Just this one time. To get it out of our systems."

"That, sweetheart, would be like jumping out of a plane without a parachute."

"It's not the fall that kills you. It's the landing."

"Now do you see?"

Suddenly he was on top of me, my wrists caught in the vise-like grip of one hand above my head, his weight pressing me into the mattress and his hard cock pressed intimately against me.

"You're not playing fair either, Asher. You talk about being decent, but it's not decent in the least for you to be wearing only my shirt and these damn granny knickers. It's not decent for you to press your hot little mouth on my neck, or to wiggle your sexy little arse against my cock." He rolled his hips, pressing his hard cock against my cleft. "It's not fair that you're in my head all the time."

Another forbidden thrill shot through me. "It's not fair that you're showing me how much you want me when you said you want to get rid of me." I relaxed my thighs so he could get even closer. I wanted him now, and I didn't care about the fallout.

"I do want to get rid of you. I can't have this." He ground his hips against me, and I arched to meet him.

He felt so goddamn good.

And so wrong.

So. So. Very. Wrong.

"You're right. You can't." This time, it was my turn to deal the killing blow.

"See?"

He rolled back down onto his side. "It doesn't matter what our bodies want."

"Doesn't it?" I couldn't catch my breath.

"Neither of us are good at playing fair. We'd destroy each other."

We would, but I couldn't help thinking it would be one hell of a way to go. I didn't actually want him. I just wanted power over him, didn't I? After all the years of... oh god, had it all been foreplay?

I didn't like where my brain was. I wasn't this person.

"This is sick. So sick," I said. But that didn't stop me from curling into him. Or from him putting his arm around me.

I don't know why I did that. I'd never get back to sleep. Every nerve ending was awake and hungry for touch and stimulation. I could see from the ridge in his pants he was still as turned on as I was.

"We're just torturing each other now."

"That's what we do best, innit?"

"It is." I licked my lips.

"You know, I'm not going to be able to help myself. I'm going to be mean as hell to you tomorrow for making me feel this. For making me talk about it and admitting this weakness out loud."

"Fine. As long as we do this again in the dark. Maybe tomorrow night, we'll see how much it hurts to kiss for real."

"I hate you," he said matter of factly.

"I hate you more," I said.

He kissed the top of my head and pulled me close, running his hands up and down the length of my back.

I touched him, too. His back, his biceps, the hard-bladed edge of his jaw.

We never kissed. We never moved our hands under our clothes. I don't know how it happened, but eventually, we slept and I knew the next day was going to bring more well-aimed arrows, but I couldn't bring myself to care as I drifted to sleep in the arms of my enemy.

Of course, when I woke up, I cared a lot.

Much to my shame and his chagrin, I'd drooled on his chest in my sleep.

I woke up with a dry mouth and my cheek in a sticky pool.

"Finally awake, are we, my little chainsaw?"

"Chainsaw?" I wrinkled my nose.

"That's what you sound like when you snore."

"It's too early for this. Can I have coffee before you start?"

"I suppose it's not at all fair since you're probably dehydrated."

I extracted myself and rubbed my eyes. The fire was still going and the sunshine was bright through the shades. Too damn bright.

I felt hungover, even though I'd only had a few beers. I guess that's what a night with Huntingdon Dane did to me.

I thought about everything that had happened and I couldn't believe how I'd behaved. The things I'd said. I'd given him so much ammo to use against me. Ammo he'd promised to use.

But he'd given me some too.

He returned with two mugs of coffee and I accepted mine gratefully. "Thanks."

We sat in silence for some time. I kept waiting for him to drop some kind of devastating bomb, but he didn't. Maybe that was part of his new plan for torture. To make me wait for the ax to fall. That was as bad as the blade itself sometimes. He was a master torturer.

"So what's on your Evil Villain Checklist today?"

"Oh, you know. Gauge the fallout from last night. See what else I can poke with a stick when we play Truth or Dare tonight. Figure out what Barclay is doing with Lauren. Trying to make you jealous would be my guess."

"Probably."

"Did it work?"

"No. He thinks you and I are together. So he doesn't owe me anything. He sure did try hard to get in my pants last night. You were right about that."

"Of course I was." He snorted. "But you're not into him now? I told you so."

"I didn't say that. I just... don't know if he's the best choice."

"Shall I continue with my plan, or not?"

"For now, yes."

"Good. The sooner the better."

I narrowed my eyes as soon as he said that, but he'd promised he'd be extra shitty today.

"Yes, the sooner the better." I gave him a sickly sweet smile and got up from the bed, grabbing my bag and heading for the en-suite shower. "I have all this sexual frustration I need to handle. The showerhead, as glorious as it is, just isn't the same as a talented tongue and a big cock."

Even as the words came out of my mouth, I regretted them. Because his eyes, I'd thought they were cold, but they weren't. They were like those blue flames. So hot they seemed cold.

I shut the door between us and turned the lock. I'd basically just told him I was going to masturbate in the shower.

What. The. Fuck.

He would, of course, give me grief about it later and in public. Wait, no he wouldn't. He'd feel like it was an assault on his prowess. Yeah, let him stew on that.

And it wasn't a lie.

I was so turned on I couldn't think straight. Maybe an orgasm would give me some control over myself again and I wouldn't find myself making out with him in that bed tonight. I wouldn't be fantasizing about fucking The Bane of My Existence™.

That was so wrong.

I heard him moving around in the room and he knocked lightly on the door. I knew he wasn't looking for me to let him in.

"What?"

"I'll be thinking about you, Cinder Girl."

Oh god, that meant he was doing the same thing I was about to do. Images slammed through my imagination hard and fast. Of him naked, his hand on his cock. Of him thinking about me while he touched himself.

I wondered most what he looked like when he let go. If even while he touched himself, if he was able to completely surrender to something he felt.

I had to bite my lip to hold back a moan. "Good."

I refused to tell him I was thinking about him, too.

And it took embarrassingly little time to reach culmination. I hadn't even started any kind of fantasy, my body was so ready for release. I shuddered as waves of pleasure washed over me with the pulsing beat of the water against my clit.

I dried off and got dressed, but even that release did nothing to stop me from thinking about what he was doing to himself.

I called through the door, "Are you decent?"

"I thought we decided last night I wasn't."

"You know what I mean."

"You mean you don't want to see the fallout?"

"I didn't know watching was an option."

"Always."

"Really?" The idea thrilled me more than it should have. "I'll call your bluff on that, Dane." I opened the door.

I was disappointed he was wearing those lounge pants. Although, he did look more rested.

I blushed and bit my lip.

"Thinking about it, are you?"

"Yeah. Don't tell me you're not."

"I am. I'll be thinking about it when I have another wank in the

57

shower." He winked at me and pushed past me into the steamy room. "And I'm really sad you didn't bring the footie jams." He closed the door in my face.

"You're just fucking with me now, Dane."

He opened the door. "If I was fucking with you, you'd know it." He closed it again with a smile.

"You do not jerk off thinking about me in my furry pajamas."

"Oh, but I do. I have. I will continue to do so," he said through the door and then the sound of the water started.

No. He was just... wasn't he?

"I know you're still there. Want to come in and watch?"

I did, but he'd already warned me things were different in the daylight. I'd wait until it was dark to get what I wanted from him.

I backed away slowly, and crept out of the room and toward the kitchen and the smell of bacon frying.

I found Barclay manning the skillets and Lauren cutting up fruit, Shae making pancakes. Bastian and Matt were sitting at the long table in the dining room and others I didn't know were outside drinking coffee and chatting. A couple guys were coming back from the lake already with a string of what looked like trout.

"Oh, dinner is looking good," Lauren said.

"Hey!" Barclay said to me. "You do bacon, right?"

"Of course." I sipped my coffee.

"Pancakes?" Shae asked.

"Everyone wants pancakes," Bastian said from the dining room.

"Wasn't talking to you," Shae called back.

"If you're talking about pancakes, you're talking to me," he corrected her.

"Can I talk to you for a sec?" Barclay asked me.

"Sure."

"Hey, Lauren. Can you man the bacon until I get back?"

"No problem."

He took my hand and led me toward another bedroom toward the back of the house.

"So. Last night," he began.

I waited for him to continue.

"How did you feel about it?"

I felt a lot of things about it, but mostly none of it had to do with him. "What do you mean?"

"Lauren."

"We didn't make each other any promises. Like, I'd expect you not to hook up with someone you liked waiting for me to be done with Dane? That wouldn't be very fair, now would it?"

I thought back to the last conversation I'd had about what was fair. Jesus, I couldn't let this thing with Dane ruin any potential future with someone else. No matter what happened with Dane, I knew it wouldn't end well. He was never someone who could be part of my future.

I didn't know if Barclay could be, but why not give him and myself a chance?

"A lot of people aren't fair when it comes to relationships, platonic or romantic. I would wait for you, you know."

Part of me didn't believe that. If he would wait, why didn't he?

"So, if you don't mind me asking, are you and Lauren together?"

"No, we're just good friends with benefits. We have been for a long time. We lost our virginity together. It was kind of a pact."

"That's the sweetest thing I've ever heard."

"Not really. It was the worst. For both of us. I'll tell you about it sometime if you want to hear the story."

"I think I do."

"And if we were to date, you know Lauren and I would still be friends."

"With benefits?"

"Not that kind. Unless you were interested in a threesome and then we could talk about it."

I snorted, but I could from his grin he was trying to lighten the mood.

He stepped closer to me and I suddenly remembered why I'd been attracted to him to begin with. His presence sucked all the air out of the space. I was light-headed and giddy.

"I want to kiss you, Asher, but I won't. At least not until tonight."

My lips felt swollen as if I had just been kissed. My tongue thick.

"What's going to change about tonight? Why will it suddenly be okay if it's not now?"

"Truth or Dare. All bets are off."

"What if I never pick dare?"

"The great thing about Lauren is that she's my ride or die. She's going to dare me to kiss you. So if you don't want me to kiss you, you shouldn't play. Fair warning."

DANE

W HEN SHE WALKED down the hall with Barclay behind her, I knew our plan was working.

It killed my insides to know our plan was working, but they needed a good dose of murder. So maybe they'd learn their place and shut the fuck up.

I lifted a piece of bacon from where Lauren and arranged it on the plate and she slapped my hand.

"Stop it."

"Worth it."

"Are you going to play tonight?" she asked me.

"Of course. It's basically my favorite thing to do."

"Playing Truth or Dare is your favorite thing to do?"

"It's like you don't even know me. It's the best way to stir shit, of course."

"I kind of thought since you've got a new girlfriend, you might not want to push those boundaries."

I took another piece of bacon and she didn't try to stop me. "Boundaries are rules. Made to be broken."

"That's kind of gross."

"Listen, I never force anything on anyone. Everyone makes their own choices. Chooses whether or not to go past their own boundaries. I simply provide opportunities."

"Hmm. Maybe I'll offer you an opportunity to push your own boundaries."

"Sweetheart, if you think you've got what it takes, give it a go."

"I might."

Shae flipped a pancake. "Lauren, you'd do better to shove a firecracker up your ass with a lit fuse than to play any game with this one." She motioned to me with her spatula.

"Does that mean you're not going to play tonight? I have something special in mind for you, so I do hope you don't chicken out."

"You think calling me a pussy is going to get me to play when I know better?"

"I do." I nodded.

She sighed. "You're right. Do your worst. I'm not afraid of you."

"Good. I'm not the one you have to be afraid of." I winked at her.

"No," Bastian called. "We should all be afraid of her and that spatula. She wields that thing like a sword."

"You're not even in here. Mind your business," Shae called.

"You are my business," Bastian snapped back.

Everyone stopped and looked from Shae to the other room and back again.

"Am not," she managed weakly.

"I guess you should take that up with him." Asher laughed and nudged Shae with her hip.

Shae rolled her eyes. "It's easier to let him think he got away with something."

"Is it?" Asher looked at me for a long moment.

"Probably," I answered.

"Is there trouble in paradise?" Barclay asked.

"Wouldn't that just thrill you to your jock strap?" I took another drink of my coffee.

"Maybe. God, I don't know how you drink it like that. I read somewhere that only psychopaths like bitter drinks," Barclay said to me.

"That's cute. I'm sure Dad will be thrilled you've started reading."

"Hey, I like my coffee black, too," Asher said. "You actually get to taste it."

"Yeah, that's the problem." Lauren poured herself a cup and cut it with cream.

"Savages," I said.

Asher and I shared a look. There was a softness in her eyes as she looked at me. I could almost feel the threads between us hardening into a steel cable that was about to tighten around my neck.

My phone buzzed in my pocket. It couldn't be anyone but my father. So I took my coffee and went outside.

"You're at the lake house with your brother?"

Obviously, he already knew. Or he wouldn't have asked. "Yes."

"He says you brought a girl with you. Who are her people?"

"Asher Warren."

"Hmm."

"Don't worry, Dad. It's not serious."

"When are you going to get serious?"

When I damn well feel like it? Fucking Cocksplat. "When you tell me who to get serious about."

I heard him exhale a sigh of relief. "Good. I was concerned you might've lost sight of the prize."

"Never. She's interested in Barclay anyway. I was simply providing her an introduction."

"Ah, still playing games with your brother. He'll never really beat you. It's like kicking a puppy."

"What did you tell me about kicking puppies? Do it often enough and they'll learn to fear the boot?"

"That's my son."

"So is Barclay." I don't know why I was being difficult. I wanted my father's approval. I needed it. I hated that I needed it, but I did.

"With his mother's softness. He's not my heir. You are. That's why I indulge him. He's doesn't need to be strong like you do. And that's why Asher Warren isn't a bad match for him. Frankly, I don't see him doing any better. Her father's a criminal, but she's shrewd. Majoring in business, isn't she?"

How did he already know that? But of course, he did. "Yes."

"See that you continue to facilitate their acquaintance."

"Anything else?"

"Not at the moment. I'll be in touch." The line went dead and I wanted to throw the phone, but I locked down my emotions and tightened my grip on it before putting it carefully into my pocket.

"I didn't mean to eavesdrop," Asher began.

"Yet you saw I was having a private conversation and listened anyway."

She bit her lip. "You're right. I did."

"Well, I'm sure you have an opinion."

"Yeah, but I can keep it to myself."

"No, by all means." I motioned for her to continue. Might as well hear it now rather than later when she was going to use it as a weapon against me.

"Your dad is a cock."

"Yeah, but he probably has this place wired, so maybe..."

"This is your father's?" She looked amused rather than concerned.

"One of them. He usually rents it out."

"You were just talking about the gauche décor..."

"You're right. He was fucking the decorator. She had terrible taste."

"Well, then."

She smiled at me and I didn't know what to do with myself.

"Yes. Well, then," I parroted, like an absolute wanker.

"So he approves of me for Barclay, but as far as you're concerned, I'm trash."

"Basically." Why lie?

"I see." She nodded slowly. "Most people in our circles think that about me now. I'm tainted by my father's crimes. I'm going to prove them wrong, though. All of them. I'll find one person to take a chance on me, and the rest of them? I'll eat them for lunch."

I understood. "You know, if you were more calculating on the personal front, I'd say to stick with Barclay. My father might be the one to take a chance on you. At least, if you're with Barclay. If you were with me, he'd try to ruin you."

She pressed her lips together as if she wanted to say something, but thought better of it. Then she said, "It's funny, isn't it?"

"What is?"

"Before my father absconded with his secretary, your father would've totally approved of us. I know for a fact that they wanted to introduce us socially. But I told my father you were The Bane of My Existence™ so he demurred."

"Did you really? That doesn't really fit with what he did, does it?"

"No, not really. But I've given up trying to understand what he was thinking. He left me. So fuck him."

"Fuck him," I agreed.

She studied me for a long time before she spoke. It was starting to unnerve me when she said, "You haven't been mean yet today. Don't keep me waiting."

"Maybe that's the mean part. Maybe I'm waiting for you to get comfortable before I strike."

"Rude." She sighed.

In that moment, I wanted nothing more than to put my arms around her. She accepted me for who I was. She hadn't asked me to be anything or anyone else. She was still here, next to me. Offering me a measure of support and comfort.

After I'd been such an utter cunt to her. And I planned on further cuntery. I'd told her square to her beautiful face. Still, she was here.

"I'm going to say something and you don't have to believe me. Because hell, what do I actually know? But you're more than your dad. You're more than his 'legacy' or whatever bullshit he's trying to feed you with a silver spoon."

No, I really wasn't. I was what my father had made me.

That look in her eyes was awful because I could see the version of me that she'd started to build in her mind. I could never live up to it and it needed to die right now. Only I couldn't bear to kill it. Not yet.

For the first time, someone saw me for something more. I both hated it and wanted it to stop as much as I needed just one more moment as something more than Huntington Dane III. Arsehole extraordinaire, Git Esquire.

"I'm really not," I confessed.

"You're anything you want to be." When I would've interrupted to argue with her, she held up her hand. "No, this isn't the part where you tell me that you're a bad man, okay? You are who you choose to be. That's all your choice. No one made you. Free will, bitch."

I wasn't supposed to laugh, but I did. I had all kinds of arguments for her, but I could tell that this was one time I'd never get the last word. At least not without pulling out the big guns, and she didn't deserve that. Not this time. Probably not any of the other times, either. But this time, I was choosing not to eviscerate her.

"Okay."

"Just okay?" she taunted. "Come on. Let it fly. I can see it on your face."

"Don't tempt me. I'm already holding back."

"Why? You don't have to hold back with me. You never did before." She crossed her arms over her chest.

"You have no idea how much I've been holding back."

She stopped and stared at me.

"But it doesn't matter," I finished.

"Fine. It doesn't matter. What does matter? Tell me something that matters. Anything."

She was pushing me again. This woman knew exactly how to push every button I had and she did it with impunity and without a thought or a care for her own safety. I was a brutal bastard because I had to be and she dared me to be worse.

"Tonight the game will matter. It's going to change everything."

"For you?"

"For everyone."

"No, I'm not letting you get away with that. You're like some great mastermind moving people around on the chessboard. Except yourself. Tell me something that really matters to you."

"No."

Damn her, but she laughed. "So it's okay to poke at everyone else's soft places but not your own?"

"I believe we already established that."

"Did we? Tell me what hurts, so I can tear it open. It won't hurt anymore."

"Do you promise?"

"I do."

"What if I like the pain?" Pain was okay. Pain was truth. It was the good things I had to hide from.

"You must." She turned on her heel and went back inside.

I couldn't tell her what hurt because it was her. The more I tried to excise her like a cancer, the deeper she thrust herself beneath my skin.

I'd already started to wonder what it would be like to be with her. To trust her. That was the stupidest thing I could do. The most dangerous.

Tonight, after Truth or Dare, she'd fall in bed with Barclay. And it would be over.

It was for the best.

I pulled out my phone and texted her.

Me: *Tonight, wear pretty knickers.*

Asher: *I only brought the grannies like you said.*

Me: *Then wear none.*

Asher: *Should I even ask?*

Me: *No.*

Asher: *Fine.*

I wouldn't think about how much it turned me on that I told her not to wear knickers and she was doing what I told her. I'd had plenty of fantasies along that route and they all ended up with her jockeying my face.

Barclay's voice sounded as he walked through the door. "Did Dad call you?"

"He did."

"I assume he was questioning you about Asher?"

He assumed? He'd already ratted me out to get what he wanted. Why act like he hadn't? "Yeah."

"He must've liked what you said. He told me not to fuck it up."

"So don't." I didn't want to have this discussion with him. I didn't want him to have Asher. And I didn't want my father scrutinizing my actions.

"I thought she was here with you," Barclay said.

"She is. I had to say I was introducing her to you. You know how he is."

"I don't understand. Do you have feelings for her, or not?" Barclay looked genuinely confused.

"Of course not. Don't be stupid. I don't have feelings for anyone."

"That sucks, Hunt. That's no way to live."

"I'll decide how I want to live, brother."

"Will you? Or will you keep letting Dad run your life?"

"Oh, as opposed to you, telling him to take his money and shove it? Wait, it didn't happen, did it?"

"No, it didn't. But as soon as I'm done with school, I will. I love him. I want to know him, but I'm not going to be his little bitch."

"Then I suggest you quit talking to Asher because he's got your future with her all planned out."

"Damn you for that, Hunt."

"Why? Are you that set on defying him that you'd stop pursuing her because he thinks she'd be good for you? You're not in middle school anymore. The time for childish rebellion is over."

"How would you know? You've never rebelled. You've always been the perfect son. The perfect heir. The perfect little Dane." Barclay scowled at me.

"That's my choice. What you do next is yours."

"Did you set this up with Dad?"

"What do you mean?"

"Don't be coy, asshole. Did you arrange this with Dad? Bringing her here."

"You're not listening. As per usual, Barclay. Didn't I just say I had to tell Dad I brought her here to meet you?"

"Does she know you told him that? Somehow, I don't think Asher would take kindly to that knowledge."

"Of course she knows. I told her."

"What did she say?"

"Nothing I'm going to repeat to you. That's our business. If you want to know how she feels about it, you ask her. If she feels like telling you, she will."

"I like her." He blurted it like it was some kind of illicit confession. Of course, he liked her.

"I knew you would."

"So what are you doing, Hunt?"

"Enjoying my time with her." And that was the truth. "We both know it's temporary."

"But why does it have to be? She seems to get you in a way that no one else does."

"That's because I made her life hell at Brewer. Know thy enemy."

"You didn't seem like enemies last night."

"There's more than one way to fight a war." I thought about the way she felt in my arms, her body pressed against mine...

"I feel sorry for you."

"That's your problem. I don't need your pity."

"You need something."

"That you don't have to offer."

"I really just want to be your brother. I think you could use a brother."

"Is this where we bond?"

"Actually, yeah. I think this is where that's supposed to happen. For those of us who actually have feelings and know what it means to be human."

"Glad I'm not one of those. Too messy. But thanks anyway."

"It's an open offer."

"I'll keep that in mind. Until then, I'm going to take the boat out."

"Are you taking Asher?"

"Maybe next time. Take care of her for me." I shouldn't have said that. I should've let it lie.

"Not a problem, brother."

I walked down to the boathouse and it wasn't long before I was on the water. It was one of my favorite places to be. There was a small bay on the north side of the lake that was fairly secluded. Only locals knew about it.

The water was clear there, with a sandy bottom and when I was a kid, I'd swim there for hours.

I liked to float in that bay. The water cradling me gently with the sun on my face and the sounds of loons in the distance. Sometimes, I could see deer on the shore.

I stayed for a long time thinking about what Asher had said about what matters. About the choices that were ultimately mine.

She was right.

Which made it all the worse. Everything I did, my father didn't force me to do. He didn't force me not to have feelings. He'd taught me the hard way how he'd use them against me.

I chose to let him.

I chose his money and security over the softer things. At least now I knew it was a conscious choice.

The easier choice.

Because I was a coward.

I was afraid to feel these things. I was afraid they'd break me. Then I'd have no one. At least this way, I had my father.

Even though I hated him.

It wasn't a good thing to realize about myself. Especially since it changed nothing.

Having this kind of epiphany should've changed something in me. It should've given me some kind of clarity or a new path. A new resolution.

But it didn't.

I was still on the same path. With the same destination.

The same stops along the way.

ASHER

He was gone most of the day, and I didn't like it. I needed to know what he was planning.

Or maybe I was just obsessing over him. That was always a possibility. Especially since I couldn't stop thinking about him. Particularly what he looked like with his hair mussed and all the things I wanted to do to muss it.

I thought I'd be happy not to see his smug face for a few hours, but I wasn't.

Even hanging with Shae.

We had breakfast together and it seemed she wanted to do anything that would keep her away from Sebastian Rathbone.

We were sitting on the dock down by lake swinging our feet in the water and eating wild blueberries we'd found when I asked her about it. "So what happened with you and Sebastian last night?"

"I've been trying not to think about it, but it's all I can think about."

"Tell me. I'm a vault. I swear, I won't say anything."

"I can't even look at Jax. I know I need to tell her what happened, but she's been persona non grata. For as much as she's decided Bastian is going to be the one, she's not spending any time with him."

"Do you think it has something to do with Matt? He seemed pretty offended that he wasn't who she chose."

"I know, right? I think just because they've been best friends for so long, Matt thought that if she was just going to pick someone to get it over with, that she might ask him."

"Or not because she didn't want to ruin their friendship? First times aren't always great."

"Yeah." She nodded. "I told them both that, but Matt said that's why she should pick him. Because he'd make sure she had a nice time. It could be a good memory they'd share, but she just shut him down cold."

"Why do you think? I wonder if she actually has romantic feelings for him?"

"Funny you should say that." Shae nodded again. "I think maybe she does too. She'd never admit it. Not even to herself, so definitely not to me. He's kind of a manwhore. In high school, he was your standard nerd. Until Senior year when his body caught up with his head and his feet. So he's been enjoying his new status as hottie and I can't blame him."

"But Jax does?"

"Basically."

"So what happened with Bastian?"

"Not getting out this, am I?"

"You don't have to tell me anything you don't want to, but I think you should talk about it with someone before you tell Jax. I mean, is she playing Truth or Dare tonight?"

"I don't know. I don't know if *I'm* playing." She bit her lip. "So something did happen, but it wasn't you know, the big thing. The main event."

I laughed and kicked my feet around. "Okay."

"Let's just say, he's a very cunning linguist."

"Oh really?" I tried not to giggle, but I failed miserably.

"Really. Like, he should have a gold medal in linguistics."

I laughed. "It sounds like you're a lucky girl."

"Don't tell Dane. He'll just...he'll fuck it all up."

"I won't say a word." I crossed my heart and then pressed my finger to my lips.

"So we were huddling for warmth, as were we all."

I nodded.

"And he just kept talking mad shit. I mean... he sang his own praises to the moon and back again. So I told him to put up or shut up."

I couldn't help it, I let out a little squeal. "Oh my god."

"I know, right? Well, he called my bluff."

"And what? He dragged you off to a cave and devoured you?"

"Basically." She turned to look at me. "Here's the thing I don't understand. He didn't get his."

"He just had lunch at the Y and left is what you're telling me."

"Yes."

"I don't understand."

"Yeah, me either."

"Well, that settles it. I'll have to dare you to blow him."

She laughed. "No."

"Why not?"

"I just... look, I'm not hung up on sex. But a blow job is relationship territory."

"Then shouldn't cunning linguistics be relationship territory, too?"

"Yes! That's my problem."

"First, can I ask why?" I was intrigued by her logic, and I wanted to know more.

"It's intimate. It's more intimate than fucking. I don't look at my vagina every day, you know? I look at my own face in the mirror all the time. I wear my face out of the house."

"One hopes."

"One does. But really... it's just always seemed more intimate to me. Just sex is fine, but putting your mouth on someone's junk, that's... it's just more."

"I ask because you're going to have to talk about what happened with him."

She looked horrified. "Why? No, I don't. I can just avoid him for the next few years."

"Is that what you want to do?"

"Yes," she squeaked.

"Liar."

"Probably."

"You don't have to decide anything now. You can let it ride, but it's going to make tonight awkward. If you're both playing."

"Why? I bet he doesn't even remember it. He's acting like nothing happened."

"What's he going to do? Get up and see you at breakfast and be like hey, that was some good eatin' last night."

"Oh. My. God." Shae started laughing so hard she was only wheezing and shaking. "I'm picturing it."

"Well. Come on."

"Okay, you're probably right."

"I'm not right very often, but the sun shines on a dog's ass twice a day and this is my hour in the sun." I smiled at her.

"I'm sure you're right more often than you think. If you weren't, you wouldn't be here with Hunt."

"Oh, I don't know about that."

"So what happened with you guys last night?" Shae asked.

"Nothing good."

She snorted. "Come on. He was so into you it was ridiculous."

"I think that was the problem? He doesn't want to be into me."

"And you don't want him to be into you because you're into Barclay? Do I have that right?"

"I honestly don't know anymore." I cringed. "I know. He's awful, but..."

"There's really no accounting for taste. On either of our parts, honestly."

"Part of me thinks I should say fuck it and go home. I feel like something is going to change tonight and I don't know if it's going to be good," I confessed.

"Oh, honey. The only thing worse than change is being stagnant. I'd rather flow to an uncomfortable place than sit and rot."

"Okay, I hope you remember that tonight."

"Oh, no using what I told you in the game." She eyed me.

"Same," I said.

We nodded in agreement together and laughed.

"I'm starving," Shae said.

"I think there's leftover pizza in the fridge."

"No, I ate it."

"That's something you and Bastian have in common. Your appetites."

"I know! If we dated it would be a big orgy of well... orgying and food. Sounds like heaven on paper." She swallowed. "I didn't say that out loud."

"No, I heard nothing."

"Good, good. Food?" Shae tilted her head.

"Yes, food. Do you have a car here?"

"No, but I'm sure we could get Barclay to take us to the resort."

"I'm kind of just enjoying girl time." No, no. I didn't want to ask Barclay. I wasn't ready to talk to him again yet.

"You could always snatch the keys to Dane's Audi."

"I wouldn't presume. Because you know what? If he took my car, I'd kill him slowly, and mine costs nothing near what his does." I tried to imagine the look on Dane's face if I just "borrowed" his car.

"That's fair."

Suddenly, the scent of grilled meat reached us.

"Oh, I wonder if they're grilling out?" Shae had picked up the scent. When it came to food, she was all apex predator. I loved that about her.

We scrambled to our feet and clambered back up the hill toward the house where we did, indeed, find Barclay and Sebastian grilling out.

"You guys have been busy," Shae said.

"Yeah, you sent out hunger pangs like a bat signal," Sebastian said.

Shae blushed. "Whatever."

"No, you really did. We were sitting here drinking some beers and thinking about doing a little waterskiing before dinner and Bastian said we better fire up the grill because you were going to be hungry and no one wanted to deal with you hungry," Barclay replied.

"I was hungry, too," Lauren said from the door. "And we ate those fish the guys caught for lunch."

"Wow, I'd love to have a friend who just knew when I was hungry and made food appear. Wouldn't you?" I asked Lauren.

"For sure." She grinned.

"Yeah," Sebastian agreed. "So are we friends, Shae?"

"Do you normally feed people you aren't friends with?" Shae asked.

"Sometimes. And sometimes they feed me." He licked his lips and Shae rolled her eyes.

I had to bite my lip not to give myself away, but I'd definitely be giving her just a smidge of shit about it later.

"Hunt took the boat out," Barclay said to me. "You must've given him a lot to think about."

"Doubtful, but it's okay. I've had a great day hanging out with Shae and getting to know everyone better. He doesn't have to babysit me."

"He'll be back in time to play. I know he doesn't want to miss this," Barclay promised me.

"I'm playing whether he's here or not." I was torn between wanting him to hurry back and wanting him to stay away.

"I like that fighting spirit," Sebastian said.

"Is there anything I can do to help?" I offered.

"Do you want to help me set the table and set out the burger dressing stations?" Lauren asked in a doubtful tone.

"Sure."

"So, Clay said you guys talked about last night."

I was a bit startled she'd just gone straight for it. "I... yeah."

"Sorry. I don't like to pussyfoot around. I feel it's better if I just tackle what I want to say head on. A lot of people don't like that about me, but I hope we can be friends."

"You can never have too many friends. Real friends, anyway."

"I think so, too. And I have to say, Clay is a real friend. He can be your friend too if you let him." She waved her hand. "I don't mean friends with benefits. I mean, if that's what you're after, sure. But I mean a real friend. You can tell him what's going on with you and Hunt. It's obvious that there's more between you than this casual thing you keep saying it is. But it's also obvious you're interested in Clay, too."

"Is this where you tell me I should pick one or you're going to make me sorry for hurting your best friend?" I watched her carefully, waiting for her reaction.

"Oh, shit no. I hate that. The best friend talk." She rolled her eyes. "It's so dumb. It's like pissing all over my territory. I don't have to do that. I know where I stand with Clay and he knows where he stands with me. Always. No, I'm trying to be your friend, too. If Clay likes you, then I like you. That means wanting you to be happy. I hope that's with Clay since he's into you. But if it's not, then it's not."

"My god, you're so self-actualized. I don't think I'm adult enough to be your friend." I wasn't exactly kidding.

"This friends with benes has taught me a lot of lessons. Mostly, how to not be an asshat, which is something we all have to learn."

"I don't know that it's something we *can* all learn."

"Oh, we can." Lauren nodded her head. "It just takes some people more time than others. And more pain than others."

I couldn't help but think of Dane. Maybe he'd already had enough of pain. From what it sounded like with his conversation with his father.

Why was I still thinking about him? I was supposed to be having fun and trying to get to know Barclay.

Maybe I was so intrigued with him because he'd told me no.

Up until my father had left, I was the only child of an investment banker. A pretty princess in a gilded cage and no wasn't something I was familiar with. After he left, I got really intimate with no and I didn't like it.

I was suddenly convinced that all Dane and I needed to get past whatever this thing was between us was to give in to it. He didn't like no either.

So if this wasn't taboo, it wouldn't hold as much fascination for either of us.

I'd tell him that tonight. Then the world could return to normal. Just where both of us liked it.

"So Barclay wants me to dare him to kiss you tonight, but I'm not going to do it unless you want me to."

"Barclay told me if I didn't want to get kissed that I shouldn't play."

"Hahaha. No. Things get intense during and after these games. A lot of feelings come to the surface that people didn't know they had. There is literally always fallout."

"It seems silly that a middle school kissing game could be that intense, but I can see why it would be now."

"So do you want to kiss Barclay, or don't you?" Lauren prompted.

"I do." Didn't I? I owed it to myself to find out.

"Anyone else you want to kiss?" She grinned at me.

"I don't know. Surprise me."

"You can bet I will," Dane said from behind us.

I turned around, and he was standing there with wet hair, and looking all warm and sun-kissed. He didn't even have the courtesy to burn like the rest of us before a tan. He'd gone out pasty white and returned looking like a golden god.

Asshole.

Had to be a spray tan. It just had to be.

"Do you promise?" I said to him, throwing his own words back at him.

"I do."

For some reason, I had the feeling I'd just countersigned my own doom.

DANE

I'D PURPOSELY CHOSEN a seat away from Asher when the game started, and the others who'd paired up had uncoupled, just like me and Asher.

Not everyone decided to play, and those who'd chosen not to went home. We were still left with a good cast of players.

Shae, Lauren, Jax, Asher, Bastian, Matt, Barclay, and me.

We gathered in the living room with after dinner beers and cocktails. Barclay was emcee.

"So if you're here, that means you've agreed to play," he began.

I noticed Asher was wearing a little yellow sundress with tiny pink flowers. It was short and I wondered if she'd followed my edict and was going commando. My mouth watered.

I took a drink of my whiskey and then another to wash away those thoughts of her, but from the way Barclay was looking at me, I rather imagined he'd decided he was going to run with the big dogs.

I guess now was the time for him to learn to stay in the shallow end of the pool.

"The rules," Barclay continued, "are as follows. Our games are what I call *mostly*. As in mostly safe and mostly sane. But they're always consensual. If the object of any dare doesn't want to participate, that is their right, but that is not without consequences. You will be removed from play. You may return for future games. No dares with penetration, except mouth to mouth kissing. No incest." He eyed everyone. "You all know Hunt is my brother. Don't make it weird. No bestiality. Etc and so forth. Things revealed during Truth turns will not leave this cabin. Or you will not be invited to play again. Does everyone understand and agree?"

Everyone nodded.

I looked at Asher and I could see she was nervous, and she should be. Tonight was going to change everything, just as I promised.

"If everyone is ready, I'll start," Barclay said. "Bastian. Truth or Dare?"

"Dare, obviously."

"I dare you to give Matt a lap dance," Barclay said.

"To what song?" Bastian was already standing up.

"*Push It* by Salt N Peppa." Shae cued up her phone.

Bastian turned toward where Matt was sitting on the couch and Matt shrugged. Jax's eyes watched them both intently. As did Asher's.

Bastian didn't hold back. In fact, I felt a little dirty for watching it, which made it that much more enjoyable.

There was some definite tension between them as Bastian moved his hips to the beat and actually crawled up into Matt's lap. These men were about the same size, both of them heavy into sports and training.

It was a homoerotic ballet of need, strength, and desire.

We were all mesmerized.

When the song was over, Matt actually blushed. "Thanks?" he mumbled.

"Yeah, thanks. For sure." Shae was breathless.

"Shit, game over. I don't think any of us can outdo that. Not with our clothes on, anyway," Lauren said.

"Happy to be of service." Bastian winked, but then he turned to Jax. "Jax, Truth or Dare?"

"Truth," she blurted. "Shit, I meant to say dare, but I'm a giant coward."

We all laughed.

"No worries. Why did you pick me to pluck your cherry instead of Matt?"

I leaned forward. Bastian went straight for the kill.

Jax looked like she'd swallowed a foot. Her own. "Jesus. Did you see yourself just now? Of course, I picked you."

"You didn't see that before you chose me," Bastian said.

"And you asked, and I answered." Jax looked terrified that no one was going to let that lie.

I could tell by the expression on Matt's face that he wouldn't.

"Shae, Truth or Dare?" Jax was quick to change the subject.

"Dare," Shae blurted. "Definitely dare."

"I dare you to answer the next phone that rings and fake an orgasm while talking to whoever it might be on the other end."

She laughed. "Yeah, okay. You all better put your shit on silent or someone's mom is going to get something they don't want."

"I don't know. I might like to hear what you sound like when you come," Matt said.

"So call me," Shae said.

Jax rolled her eyes.

"Asher, Truth or Dare?" Shae said.

"Dare?" She cringed. "God, it's all going to be horrible."

"I don't know about that." Shae eyed her. "I dare you to sit in Hunt's lap for the rest of the game, unless you're performing a dare or he is."

"You're mean, you know that? I'm going to get you," Asher promised.

And it made me smile.

Until she slid onto my lap. From the heat coming through my slacks, she definitely wasn't wearing panties. She squirmed against me and I put my arm around her so I could hiss in her ear. "Stop that. You know where that gets us both."

She stilled.

"Matt, Truth or Dare?" Asher asked.

"Dare."

"I dare you to make out with Bastian. I think we all needed a little more of that," Asher said.

Her dare surprised me, but it shouldn't have. She was going to make Shae wait for her punishment.

Matt blushed but went over to Bastian. "This cool?"

Bastian grinned and kissed him hard. They wrapped around each other and there was definitely tongue. When they were done, Matt looked all kinds of fucked up.

"Lauren, Truth or Dare?" The words stumbled out of his mouth like drunk frat boys.

"Dare."

"Make out with Asher, but she stays in Hunt's lap."

Well, if I had to die, I guess this was as good of a way as any to go. Maybe the best, really.

Lauren smiled and came over to us. She whispered in my ear, "You can touch too, if you want."

Asher leaned over and met Lauren halfway, their mouths colliding.

I think everyone in the room held their breath because no one wanted to be a wheezing mouth-breather. Watching them make out was as hot as watching Bastian and Matt.

When Lauren's hand moved to Asher's breast, we all gasped, but Asher was totally lost.

Yeah, call me a pig, but I'd be storing this up to think about often.

They broke apart, and then they turned on me. Like wild dogs on prey. Lauren kissed one side of my mouth and Asher the other.

I'd had threesomes before. They were mostly passé at this point in my life, but something about these two women together was fire.

The three of us broke apart when Barclay finally said, "Hunt gets all the fun."

"I wouldn't say that," Lauren answered. "Your turn."

"What's my dare?" Barclay asked.

"Kiss Asher." She grinned. "I mean, when something's that good, you just have to share with your bestie." She winked at him.

Barclay looked at Asher and raised a brow.

This was the moment I'd been conspiring to bring about. Yet, as it was being born, there was a part of me that would've done absolutely anything to stop it. I watched silently as she sauntered over to him and he pulled her down into his lap. He bent her back in some ridiculous pose and kissed her.

Her arm twined around his neck and Barclay deepened the kiss. I think after a solid minute, it could be classified as making out. Not just kissing.

"Jesus, Barclay. Leave some for someone else," Shae said. "What? Everyone was thinking it."

He finally released her and she blinked, her lips swollen and bee-stung. She looked dazed, but still, she got out of his lap and wandered back over to me, where she sank down in my lap.

Much to my displeasure, I was still hard.

Her head whipped around so she could look me in the eyes.

I schooled my features so that I gave nothing away. No displeasure. No need. Nothing.

She squinted, as if that would help her see something that wasn't there. That I refused to let be there.

"Hunt hasn't had a turn," Shae said.

"Yeah, I'm getting to that." Barclay smiled. "He likes to talk about his prowess. I'd like to see him prove it."

"I haven't even chosen dare, yet, mate."

"But you will, won't you?" Barclay prompted.

"Of course." Truth was a weapon that could be used against anyone, but I kept those to a minimum for myself. Making out with anyone, up to and including slobbing a knob was less dangerous.

"Make Asher come without removing a single piece of clothing."

"I already did that this morning."

Asher blushed and turned her face into my shoulder.

"What is this, the Asher show? You've singled her out," I said.

"Never in your life have you defended another living being. So you must not be able to do it." Barclay gave me a smug look.

"You're not listening, Barclay. I said I already did it this morning."

"It's okay," Asher whispered in my ear. "Do it. If you can."

"The lady consents, so what else can I do?" I gave my brother a hard glare. I'd make him pay for this. Oh yes, I would.

I gave her my chair and knelt between her knees.

"You said not to remove any clothes. Good thing I told her not to wear knickers today."

I pulled her to the edge of the seat and she didn't resist me at all. What a little exhibitionist she was.

I pressed my mouth to her cleft and she cried out even as her nails dug into my forearms.

The room was silent at first, until Asher, not shy at all about what she liked, moaned and gasped. It was as if that was tacit permission for everyone else to breathe. And to be turned on by what was happening in front of them.

Shae said, "Holy shit, I see what the fuss is about now."

"Me too," Jax squeaked.

Yeah, Barclay had fucked himself there. He could've been in the bedroom with Asher, but now, it was me who was tasting her. Me who was making her dig her nails into my arm and demand more.

And it was me who made her come.

Only I didn't stop. She hadn't told me to stop. I felt her body convulse, I tasted the evidence of her pleasure, but instead of stopping, I eased back, only to continue manipulating her with my tongue and as promised, not penetration.

"Jesus Christ, Hunt," she whimpered.

But I took no pity on her, for I had none. All I had was the taste of her on my lips, and the memory of what she felt like while her body shuddered with bliss.

Finally, she slapped my arm. "I'm done, shit, I'm done."

I wasn't. I could do that all day. But I pressed a chaste kiss on her inner thigh, and then as she righted her dress, one on her lips.

She didn't shy away.

In that moment, I was sure all my plans had just shat the bed, but I didn't care. I needed Asher Warren, and tonight, I was sure she was going to give me everything I wanted.

"I volunteer as tribute?" Lauren said, blushing.

I gave her a lazy half-smirk. "Any time. You can join us tonight, if Asher's game."

Asher didn't say anything, and from the dazed look on her face, I don't think she even heard what was said.

"Hmm. My turn." I licked my lips and scanned the group. "Shae. Truth or Dare?"

"Dare?"

"You don't sound sure. Is it a question or an answer?"

"An answer, I guess. But I don't know what you could possibly dare me to do that's within the rules that could top that? This game has been hardcore from dare one."

"You know that's how we all like it, whether we admit it or not," I said. "I dare you to strip naked for the whole of the next turn."

"If you wanted to see me naked, Hunt, all you had to do was ask," she said, but began to strip off her clothes.

"I just did."

Bastian's eyes were drawn to her, as were we all. But he took extra care not to look.

"Jax, Truth or Dare?" Shae asked, unmindful of her nakedness.

"Dare."

"I dare you to skinny dip."

"Where?"

"Right there. Down off the dock." Shae pointed.

Pressing her lips together, she got up and headed for the sliding glass doors that led outside. She stripped off her clothes one item at a time as she walked down to the lake.

"Everyone!" Barclay called.

We followed suit like a bunch of sheep. All stripping down by the shore and wading into the water, naked.

We were all swimming, paddling around, when Asher waded toward me. "Is that it? Is the game over?"

"Yeah. We basically won. I mean... no one could really top that. Anything after was going to seem silly."

"I... thank you?" She blushed.

"For what?"

"You know."

"Making you come so hard you ripped the skin off my arms? You're welcome. You can hold my hand in surgery if I get a parasite from this lake water in my open wounds."

She laughed. "You've got a deal."

Her eyes cast downward, her lashes brushed her cheeks. I wanted her to look at me.

"What's wrong?" I asked before I could stop myself. This was out of character for me. I shouldn't be asking her what was wrong. I shouldn't care. I definitely shouldn't want.

"Nothing. I have something to tell you."

"Is it a government secret? Tell me."

"No. Tonight. Later."

"Why not now? You know I hate surprises." I reached out and put my hand on her waist to draw her closer. Her breasts brushed against my naked chest.

Then she did look up at me. What I saw in her eyes was nothing short of terrifying. I knew what she was going to say.

She was right. I didn't want to hear it. I couldn't hear it now.

Maybe in the dark where such secrets were kept, it would be okay.

I kissed her forehead. "Yes. Later."

And I fled like a little bitch.

I swam out toward deeper water, away from my splashing friends.

Too bad my bastard brother followed me.

"You win, Hunt."

No, I hadn't won anything. Not really.

"I usually do," I said.

"When are you going to tell her she'll never be good enough for you?"

"She already knows about my conversation with the illustrious Huntington Dane II. I told you, I don't lie. I certainly wouldn't lie to her when it could so easily be turned against me."

"You brought her here. You obviously wanted me to make a play for her, but then..."

"Oh, don't turn this on me. You're the one who dared me to make her come. What did you think was going to happen?"

"I don't know. Shit. I got caught up in the game."

"Lesson learned, right brother?"

"Yeah. Lesson learned."

ASHER

HE BASICALLY RAN AWAY from me.

But it was okay. He'd agreed to listen to me tonight. He knew what I was going to say to him and it would be okay when we were lying next to each other in the dark. When the waking world was hidden away as were the fake shells of ourselves. At least that's what I kept telling myself.

I couldn't believe I'd let him eat me out in front of a crowd of people, but hey, that's what college was for, making mistakes.

Except, I didn't think it was a mistake.

It felt good. Nothing that felt that good could be a mistake.

It was nice to have eyes on me that were envying me instead of judging me. That didn't mean I wanted to be the main event at every show time, but just that once.

Then there was the perverse part of me that was thrilled to have Huntington Dane paying homage to my clit using his foul tongue for good.

I swam around for a bit, enjoying the cool bite of the water, laughing with Shae and Lauren until the sun started to set on the horizon and the chill in the water turned into a snap in the air.

We all trudged back to the house and I offered to make everyone hot cocoa. We hugged and promised we'd be better friends back at school.

Everyone except Dane.

I showered and crawled into bed, waiting for him.

For a moment, I wondered if he'd just decided to skip this part. If he didn't want to hear what I had to say after all. If he didn't actually have any of the same feelings and this had all been some kind of trick.

Finally, the door creaked open. "You still awake?"

"Yeah."

"Good. I'm going to shower. If you still want to talk, we can talk when I'm done."

I summoned my courage. "I don't actually want to talk anymore."

"What do you want?" He paused outside of the bathroom door.

"You."

I didn't know what he was going to say, if he was going to say anything at all.

"That would be a mistake," he said finally. "For both of us."

"I know."

"And you're sure it's a mistake you can live with?" He took a deep breath. "Because I'm not sure I can, Asher. I'll confess something. I told you I never lie, but that wasn't the truth."

The moonlight shone on his blond hair, making him look almost like an angel, but that was a lie, too. Unless this was really hell, like I'd thought the first time. He was silent for a long time.

I finally said, "Truth or Dare, Hunt?"

"Truth," he said quietly. "I'm not on a budget. I just needed to get you the hell away from me."

"Why?"

"Why do think? Because I can't stop thinking about you. Because I want you and I can't have you and it's making me insane."

"Is that why you've been an always been an absolute shit to me?" I was incredulous.

"No. I used to just be a shite. But when I saw you at Winter Royalty in that blue dress, it changed everything."

"You smiled at me that night. A real smile. And it almost killed me. I thought that was your evil plan." I remembered it like it was yesterday. He was wearing this tux and looked GQ gorgeous, and I'd wanted to gouge out my own eyes for having seen him like that. Or for thinking he was even remotely attractive.

"Yeah, that's when I knew you were dangerous." He closed the door slowly. "You have all the power now, Asher."

"I really don't. It doesn't have to be this way. We can learn to trust each other. I don't want to hurt you. And you don't want to hurt me, right?"

"Oh, but I do. I have to hurt you before you can hurt me."

"That's a terrible way to live."

"It's a safe way to live. I've told you who I am. The next move is yours. Truth or Dare, Asher?"

I wanted to say dare, but I wasn't ready yet. I thought I was, but I needed... I didn't know what I needed. More guts, probably. "Truth."

"What do you really want from me?"

Part of me wanted to say that I just wanted him to come fuck me so we could both get it out of our systems, but that wasn't the whole truth. I wanted him. All of him. But I was scared of it, too. I didn't know if I was strong enough.

"Just you."

"Then damn us both."

"Truth or Dare?" I whispered.

"Dare."

"I dare you to give me everything I want."

He peeled off his shirt and my mouth went dry, my stomach curled into knots. Oh my god, this was happening. How did we get here? I blinked and my whole life, my whole set of ideas about how the world worked had changed.

When we went back to Ridgemont Hall, we wouldn't be the same people. We'd be... this new incarnation of us. Us that wasn't really us.

Shit, I was overthinking it before it even happened.

I was like some kind of trembling virgin waiting for her fate.

No, fuck that. I pulled the covers back and rose up to my knees, crawling toward him on the bed.

"Kiss me, Hunt. Kiss me like you mean it."

"I do." His hands threaded through my hair, but instead of kissing me, he rested his forehead against mine.

My heart was about to explode out of my chest, but I let myself wait. I let myself be present in this moment before everything changed again. Our breath mingled, our lips as close as they'd ever been, but farther somehow.

"It's not often you get to know before something happens that it's going to change you forever. Usually, those things just happen. You look back on it and you're like, that was it. The moment."

"You think this is a moment?"

"Don't you?"

I bit my lip and tightened my arms around him. "Yeah, I know it is."

"I'm scared, Cinder Girl."

His use of the name didn't make me angry any more. He'd just trusted me. Just shown me a side of himself I didn't think he'd shown to anyone else.

"Me too."

"I think you want more from me than what I can give you. I know you said you just want me, but I...fuck it. I'm the bad guy, right? You're not a princess in need of saving and you told me you don't want a knight in shining armor. I'm going to take you at your word so I can have what I want."

"What we both want."

Yet still, he didn't kiss me. Still, he was trying to save me. Or maybe it was himself he tried to save.

I closed the distance left between us and pressed my lips to his softly.

It was silly that after he'd had his mouth between my legs that kissing was still so intimate, so forbidden a thing between us, but it was.

And I wanted more.

More of his hands in my hair, more skin to skin contact, more of everything.

"Asher." His voice was husky in my ear as his mouth moved to my throat, a hot trail down to my collarbone and then back up to my mouth.

Then I did the same to him, remembering how just the touch of my lips on his neck had caused an immediate retaliatory reaction.

I was suddenly flat on my back and he was on top of me like last night, but he didn't hold my hands above my head. I was free to touch him anywhere I desired.

I didn't hesitate. I went straight for his belt.

He reached over toward something on the nightstand. "Condoms," he mumbled against my lips.

I made some noise of agreement, I think. My whole body was on fire. I couldn't think, all I could do was feel.

Somewhere that seemed a hundred miles away, I heard the tear of the wrapper and he reached down between us.

Then he was inside me.

A sensation unlike any I'd ever known uncurled from my belly and stretched long tendrils into my limbs. The thought sounded so faux porn even in my own head, but I had literally never felt so... much. So full. So connected. So good.

One hand cupped my cheek. "Open your eyes," he said.

I couldn't. My lids were so heavy, I was dizzy with need. But I finally did and when I looked into his eyes, that was when he began to move.

I'd always thought people who did that we were weird. Opening my eyes to see my partner looking at me while doing that weird fuck over-bite was not what I considered hot. With Hunt, it wasn't like that. It made everything more intense.

And he didn't make stupid faces, either.

Or maybe I didn't care because this seemed like the most intimate I'd ever been with another person. He was inside me, but these moments looking into each other's eyes, I was inside him, too.

When he kissed me again, I knew I'd been ruined for anything else. Maybe even any*one* else.

I pushed that thought out of my head.

It was just Good D.

Even as I thought it, something cold washed over me, and I pushed that away too.

"Where'd you go? Stay here with me."

"I'm not going anywhere," I promised.

"Good. I'm not done with you yet. Not by a long shot." He withdrew from me and I cried out. "Don't worry. I said I wasn't done."

He leaned back against the headboard and hauled me on top of him.

"I want to look at you."

I put my hands on his shoulders and straddled him, taking him even deeper than he'd been before.

"Fucking hell, you're beautiful." He cupped my breasts, his thumbs working my taut nipples.

"Tell me again." I rolled my hips and worked my body against his.

"You are beautiful, my Cinder Girl."

For a moment, I felt it. I felt like the most beautiful woman on earth. Something treasured. Wanted. Maybe even needed.

I'd never doubted that I was a pretty girl. My features fit together in a pleasing way. I didn't hate looking in the mirror. But Dane had made me feel ugly. When he reminded me of all my flaws and faults, I felt like less.

I knew I shouldn't have needed his validation, but need or not, I wanted it. It felt good to have it.

"You know," he teased, "this is where you tell me how hot I am, too."

"There's a difference between hot and beautiful."

"Only you would want to argue at a time like this."

"Something about you, Dane."

"So it's back to Dane, now, is it?"

"Maybe. I've always been Cinder Girl."

"But you like it now." He flashed me a devastating smile. "Don't even try to say you don't."

"Stop talking." I kissed him.

"No. Not until you tell me I'm pretty, too."

"You're a vain little peacock, aren't you?"

"Like you're not? And little? Where have you been?"

I blushed. "Yeah, okay. You're not little." I shifted my hips again and clenched around his cock.

He made a sound low in his throat. "So good, Cinder Girl. So good."

"Maybe I'll let you talk. So you can keep singing my praises."

His hands anchored to my hips and he guided me to meet his upward thrust. But then he stopped.

"Tell me the truth, Asher."

"About what?" I gasped. I'd have told him anything in that moment just to keep him moving.

"I'll stroke you anywhere you like with anything you like, and all you have to do is stroke me back where I asked. Tell me."

"Fine, fucker. You're beautiful. You've got cheeks like blades, eyelashes like gold filigree and I thought your eyes were Antarctica, but they're not. They're so hot they seem cold. You're like Jack Frost brought to life as a GQ Fuck Me Ken Doll. And your cock should have a leash because it's a beast. There? Are you happy?"

He thrust up again and I shuddered.

"Yes. Mostly."

"What else do you want from me?" I needed to get closer to him, needed more friction, more skin.

More of him.

"For you to come."

Our mouths crashed together in a kiss, and it was no slow seduction this time. It was all lightning.

I was sure I was going to die. This sensation built inside of me and... yeah, I knew what orgasms were, but it had never been like this.

It was like my whole body imploded, then exploded and all the pieces of myself were slowly drifting back together like mercury.

I found myself curled into him, his fingers drawing lazy circles on my lower back.

"A Jack Frost Fuck Me Ken Doll, huh?"

"Shut up."

"Oh, I'm never going to let you forget that, Cinder Girl. Never ever." He laughed.

"Yeah, well you think I'm beautiful, too. You said so. With no prompting, I might add."

"You have a mirror. It's not news."

"But it is. At least, that you think so."

"Tomorrow, we go back to Ridgemont," he reminded me.

"Yeah."

We were both silent. I didn't know what to say and I was pretty sure he didn't either. Obviously, this wouldn't be a thing when we went back to the real world.

"I guess attempt number one to get rid of me failed," I said, finally.

"Spectacularly."

His answer pissed me off. I guess I wanted him to say that he didn't want to get rid of me. That he wanted to try this thing between us, to see where it went. I think I wanted him to say he'd fall with me. Even though we'd hit rock bottom and break ourselves, that it would be worth it.

But he'd never say that.

He'd never think that.

I had no reason to be angry. I knew what I'd signed up for, but it still stung in ways I didn't want to examine. I pulled away from him and rolled over.

"Oh, are we done now?" His voice was strangely distant.

I didn't say anything. What was I going to say to that? Why drag it out anyway? Tomorrow we'd back to our regular scheduled positions on the opposite sides of a war neither of us would ever win.

"Kiss me goodbye," he said.

I was wrapped in his arms again, and it felt so right, it hurt. Because I knew this couldn't happen again.

It wouldn't. He was about to be the biggest asshole in the history of Hollingsworth University. He'd do it to put distance between us. Between this thing we felt together. To break it.

And maybe break me. He'd said as much.

Fuck if I'd let him break me because he was afraid of feeling something.

Then it occurred to me, why should I let that stop me from feeling? Because it was going to hurt?

Fuck it. Life hurts. But it feels good, too. There are moments of beauty and bliss that make it all worth it. That was a lesson I'd already learned.

So I turned into him. "No, we're not done yet. I thought we were, but there are still hours left of darkness, and this is our time, isn't it?"

"Oh, Cinder. You're going to burn us both up, aren't you?"

I kissed him like he'd asked, and I jumped. I let all the feelings I was afraid of have me. It was like throwing myself to a pack of wolves, and when dawn came and it hurt to sit down, hurt to cross my legs, and sometimes, it even hurt to breathe, I knew I'd made the right choice.

I'd never be able to think of Bear Lake again and not remember my night with Huntington Dane.

And neither would he.

Our night together had wrecked us both in more ways than one.

DANE

It finally happened.

I'd had ALL of the sex and there was none left for anyone else.

I was also going to die. Death by dehydration. My cock had never been this sore, yet I wanted her again. Maybe because I knew this was a finite prospect, as was everything.

Only you don't go into relationships thinking, "This is temporary. I'll only get to kiss this woman x number of times. We only have x number of sunrises together." Which is true. Even if you're happily married, it doesn't last forever. Someone dies. We all do eventually.

A morbid way to look at it, I know.

I'd been taught to see everything as temporary. Except money and power.

Last night, when she'd turned away from me, it had hurt, but it had been for the best. What had happened after had been nothing short of stupid, but I'm glad we'd done it.

I watched her carrying a cast-off bit of my luggage, wearing yet another of my shirts, and hugging all of our new friends goodbye with promises to keep in touch back at Ridgemont Hall. To really be friends. Most of these friendships only lived and breathed at these parties, the fire in them dwindled to embers back at school, but then blazed to life again.

Except I knew that Asher meant it.

For a moment, my brain played out a scenario I had no business thinking about. That this would be what it was like to be with her. Not just what happened last night, but this morning too. Coffee and bacon together in bed. Making every second last as long as possible.

The way she looked back at me when she thought I wasn't paying attention.

It could be perfect. Well, as perfect as any two humans together could be. Except for my father.

Barclay held out his hand to me, interrupting my thoughts. "Glad you came, brother."

My first instinct was to reply with, "Are you really?" But I didn't. Instead, I just took his hand.

And this fucker yanked me into a "frat boy" hug. Where it starts as a handshake but then you sort of bump shoulders and smack each other on the back.

"What fresh hell is this?" I hissed at him.

"I love you, Hunt. It's time for all this childish bullshit to come to an end, don't you think? Let's really be brothers. Me and you against the world."

"And all I have to do is stop seeing Asher?"

"What is actually wrong with you? Maybe that's a play you'd make, but not me. I'm done with the one-upmanship. It would be one thing if this was good-natured competition, but it's not. I know I started it when I slept with Pandy, but she bears some blame here, too. She's the one who made you a promise. I didn't even know you were together."

Wasn't it maybe time to let go of that? It had been years and I'd never loved Pandy. I thought I had, with all the intensity of a child. This thing with Barclay was more habit now than anything.

It galled me that he wasn't that bright, but he was ahead of the game on this.

"Jesus Hunt, you look like you just drank sour milk. The idea of being brothers is that abhorrent to you?"

"I appreciate your use of abhorrent. And no, I'm just irritated you thought of it first."

Barclay laughed. "So do you want to try this brothers thing? Because I do. I always have."

"Fine. Whatever."

He hugged me again and I wanted to rip my skin off. I wasn't used to physical affection. Touching to fuck was one thing, but touching just to touch was something altogether new and awful. I didn't like it.

But I slapped at his back awkwardly. "Yeah, okay."

I could feel Asher's eyes on us and when I looked up, she smiled at me. I had to tell her to stop doing that. I liked it too much.

I disengaged from Barclay and I went over to her. "I'll take your bag to the auto, if there's anyone else you want to say goodbye to before we leave."

"Such a gentleman."

"Nice to be recognized for solid work."

She laughed again. "God, I'm going to miss you."

Her words punched me in the gut. "Doubtful. You're going to see me in the pod."

"I guess I will." Her wistful tone was full of something else. "I need to say goodbye to you, and I know I should've done that last night, but maybe we can walk each other to our doors. You know. It's polite."

"It is. And we were both raised with impeccable manners. I'm glad to see you using yours." We were being twats about this, dragging it out. I knew I should be the one to say we were done. We didn't need to walk each other anywhere, but maybe we did. Maybe she did.

Maybe I did.

She snorted. "I'm going to grab a diet coke for the road. Do you want anything?"

I remembered last night, asking her what she wanted from me. The way she'd looked at me. How she said she just wanted me.

I was tempted to tell her the same, but I knew better.

"No, thank you. I'll be in the auto."

I walked out to the Audi without looking or speaking to anyone else. For the first time, I didn't want to push my pretty little machine to her and my limits. I didn't want to go back to Hollingsworth and my real life at all.

And why did I have to?

I was Huntington Dane III. I could have whatever I wanted. So why couldn't I have her?

You know the answer to that, you twat. Because you want her too much.

I had to admit that Asher and Barclay were both right on that. Living without what you really wanted because you were taught to fear losing it was miserable.

Had my father ever gone a day in his life without something he wanted? Barclay was living, breathing proof my father didn't hold himself to any kind of standard. So why should I?

Because my father would shred Asher Warren.

I knew she was strong, but she was still soft on the inside. Maybe she always would be, but my father would tear her apart. Someday, she'd be an opponent who could hold her own with him, but she wasn't yet.

I wasn't yet.

Even if I was willing to rebel for her, it wouldn't really be for her, would it? It would be for me and I'd be dropping her right into the jaws of the lion.

At least she wasn't interested in Barclay anymore. As much as I'd plotted and planned to get them together, that would've been worse than any other hell I could've devised for myself.

Asher slid into the auto. "Sorry about stealing all of your clothes. Your shirts are comfy."

I liked seeing her in them. "I didn't notice. Wear them any time you like."

"Even when we get back to reality?"

"Even then."

She bit her lip and looked for a moment like she was going to cry. Except she smiled, and the worst part of that was that it wasn't real. I'd have done almost anything in that moment to take away whatever was hurting her.

But it was me.

"Or not. Christ, if it's going to make you cry."

"You're not supposed to notice that."

"All apologies, Cinder Girl. You know, you don't always have to be the dragon. You can be the princess."

"Being the princess never brought me anything but trouble. I'd rather breathe fire, thank you very much."

"Me too."

"As if you were the princess." She snorted. "I'd love to see you in your dress for the ball."

"Princes are allowed to need saving too, you know."

"But they're not allowed to admit it?"

"Wouldn't you say that's toxic masculinity?"

"Well, it is. But isn't that your thing?" She arched a brow.

"No. I was taught it's weakness for anyone to show their feelings. Not just men."

"Maybe it is. Or maybe it takes more strength to be vulnerable."

"I'm sure it does. It's a strength I don't have," I admitted.

"Me either."

"So, we're both dragons. Fine with me."

She laughed and this time, it was real. "What do dragons eat for lunch?"

"Are you hungry already?"

"I'm just planning ahead."

I thought about all the places we could've gone instead of back to Hollingsworth, but in the end, I did what I knew to be for the best.

I drove back to the university.

When we got back to the pod, I realized we'd missed the annual key party, when I saw the flyers hanging around the common room.

"Glad we missed this. I have zero interest in hooking up with some rando from the Hall," she said.

"Same for me as well. I wonder who Pandy and Conrad ended up with?"

"I guess we'll find out."

A look passed between us. Obviously, neither of us really wanted to know.

"What if they got each other's keys?" she snickered.

"Oh, now I'm sad I missed it. That would be something I would go to great lengths to arrange. It would be interesting to see them turn their powers on each other."

"I know, right?" Asher cackled. "That's just what they deserve."

"Let's not go too far down that road about what others deserve." I eyed her.

She shrugged. "Karma's only a bitch if you are."

"And I am," I reminded her.

She cackled again. Full on wicked witch style. I liked that about her. I liked way too many things about her.

"So does this count as the real world, yet?"

"I don't know. I don't think we can really count it until Monday."

"I was hoping you'd say that." The tight set to her shoulders relaxed.

"Did you decide what dragons eat for lunch?"

"Pizza, of course."

"Not sushi or French? But pizza?"

"Yep." She was adamant. "From that place downtown. And wings. My treat."

For a second, I thought she was speaking another language. "Your. Treat. I don't understand what that means."

"Shut up, Dane. Yes, you do. It means I buy." She held up her hand. "And I don't want to hear anything about it."

"Love, whyever in the world would I let you do that? You work too hard for your money and it's literally falling out of my arse. Let me pay."

"No. It's because I work hard for it that it matters that you just go with it."

If I thought my skin was itchy before, now it was practically crawling off my body. She wanted to buy me lunch.

Me.

Huntington Dane III.

Who bought anything and mostly anyone he wanted. I always paid. It was an automatic response. Whenever I was out with any friends, girlfriends, anyone. I paid. I didn't care about the money one way or another.

Asher Warren, who had once lived life the same way, who worked in the sodding cafeteria which was as thankless a task as they come, wanted to pay for me.

No, this water was way too deep. We were both going to drown.

Instead of saying so, I just nodded. Like a fucking muppet.

I could admit, it was the best pizza I'd ever had. I'd never tasted anything quite like it. A meal that I hadn't paid for had a unique flavor.

And I'd never known anyone quite like Asher, either.

When we were lying together in my bed later, she said, "I really want to do more than sleep, but I think I'm way too sore."

"Oh good. Because I was going to have to say that I'll just have to take a raincheck and for my part. I'm happy to have dessert, love, but the rest of me isn't able. Yet."

"Can we do that?"

"Sure." I pounced on her ready, willing, and able to bring her off with my mouth again.

"God, not that." She squirmed away from me and crossed her legs. "No, not that."

I was confused. "Then what?"

"The raincheck part. I know you don't want to date me any more than I want to date you, but maybe this could happen again." She coughed. "No strings."

But there were strings. There were so many strings it was an army of goddamn harps.

"So, what, you just want to creep to each other's rooms with a battle cry of 'rain check, bitch.'"

She laughed. "Maybe not so brutal, but it could be a code. Maybe you see me in my 'footie jams' as you call them and I just say, 'Raincheck tonight.' And you say yes or no."

"If you're sure you want that."

"Never repeat this, and I know you will. You'll remind me every chance you get, but you were right."

"I never get tired of being right."

"Of course you don't."

"What was I right about? Besides everything?" I asked her.

She snorted. She did that a lot when she was talking to me. I found it incredibly and disgustingly adorable.

"About one time not being enough."

"I think we blew that out of the water with the eight times last night, don't you think?"

"Well, I mean, that counts as one session, right?"

"I see what you mean. Yes."

"I'm not ashamed to admit, I need more. I think you do, too. And no feelings isn't hard for you. You've got this wonderful switch that I wish I could install in myself. You just flip it and off you go."

Her words were cold water on my face. I thought she knew me better than that. Maybe she did. Maybe she was daring me to flip my switch. After all, I'd already told her about I-Dare-You-To-Care Syndrome. She knew.

"What about your feelings?"

"Those are my problem. They've never bothered you before."

She was right about that. I never stopped to think about what I was doing to her. Or how it would make her feel. Why start now?

Even as I said those words to myself, I knew that last part was a lie. I was already in too deep.

It wasn't that I couldn't resist her offer, it was that I didn't want to.

"Okay. We agree to raincheck privileges. Since we're negotiating, what about parties?"

"I think we know how that's going to end up."

"But in the interim, we're both free to sleep with other people?"

She exhaled before she spoke. "I'm not going to even try to lie. This is my vulnerable moment, so don't laugh?"

"I won't," I swore to her. And I meant it.

"I don't want to agree to that. I know it's completely unreasonable. We're not dating, but I don't want to share you. I don't want you to want to share me."

"You seemed pretty into it with Lauren."

"That was different. I was included."

"So... what do you want?" I shouldn't even have asked this question.

"I think the question is what can I have?"

"You can have anything you want," I blurted before I could think better of it.

"Anything I want?"

"I told you. You have the power here."

"No, your father has the power."

She was right about that. At least for now.

"For the sake of keeping our feelings detached, we should probably not put any restrictions on ourselves." I didn't even like saying the words.

"I know, but that doesn't change how I already feel about it."

"The way I was raised is if something's uncomfortable, we don't talk about it. We could do that with this, too."

"Deal," she said. "Don't tell me. I won't tell you." She scooted off the bed. "I'm going to get a water. Do you want one?"

"Yeah. The top right of the fridge are sparkling, if you want one."

I watched her arse as she left my room.

But then I heard Pandora's voice. "What. The. Actual. Fuck. Why are you wearing Hunt's shirt? Why is he... oh my god." She sounded like a startled goose.

"Why am I..." Then Asher cackled. It was one of pure malicious glee. "Why is Conrad naked in your room?"

ASHER

I THINK it was the first time I'd ever seen Pandora Heyde at a loss for words. It was a good look.

Or maybe it was just because she hadn't straightened her hair. Her natural hair was beautiful, but I'd rather die a thousand horrible deaths than tell her that.

"It was the key party. It means zero."

"Nothing means anything to you. That's the sad part."

"Oh fuck off, Cinder." Pandora rolled her eyes.

"He calls me that while we're fucking now, so it doesn't really have the same bite." It gave me way too much joy to drop that bit of information on her.

"It will when he gets tired of you. Or when Daddy gets tired of you for him. You'll go back to being the girl scrounging in the ashes."

I lifted my chin. "Maybe. But you know what? I'm really good at holding a grudge. I also know what it means to have to fight for what I have, and I'm hungry, *Pandy*. You don't know what it's like to be hungry. So you won't be able to fight with the same ferocity. I'll take everything away from you if you keep pushing me. Maybe not today. Maybe not tomorrow. But the someday when you're least able to defend yourself, I'll tear your throat out."

Conrad clapped from the bedroom. "I've been waiting forever for you to fight back. Told you."

Pandora rolled her eyes. "That would be sad, wouldn't it? To spend all that time and effort to pay me back because I hurt your little feels."

"No sadder than 'hurting my feels' because mommy and daddy don't pay enough attention to you."

"Can we please just not, right now?" Conrad came to the door. "This is awkward for all of us. Why don't we just pretend this didn't happen? Like, literally? We're all having an off weekend doing things we'd never normally consider. Let's just get our San Pellegrinos and return to our respective corners until tomorrow. Oh, and we'll never mention any of this again. To anyone. Ever. Especially not each other."

"Hmm, I think maybe you might have something there, Conrad. That's why we have the key party anyway. To keep our indiscretions in-house. Are you game?" Pandora asked me.

I had more important things to worry about at the moment than who Pandora Heyde was fucking. So I agreed. "Fine."

"Good. See you back when the world makes sense." Conrad sauntered back into the depths of Pandora's room.

"Great pate, gotta motor if I want to be ready for that tour in hell." Pandora turned on her heel.

Heathers references. Apropos. Pandora would be funny if she wasn't such a thundercunt.

I grabbed the waters and went back into Hunt's room. "So that happened."

"It could've gone much worse, really. If we're rainchecking, it was bound to happen sooner or later."

He was right. We wouldn't have been able to keep that from them long. I wondered briefly how that conversation would've gone. What he'd have said about me to her.

Sometimes I like to fuck the help.

I tried not to think about it, but it had started playing on a vicious loop in my head. So I gave in and asked him.

Not until later though, when we were in bed for the night and it was dark. "Truth or Dare?" I whispered.

"Well, neither one of us is up to dare, so I imagine you want me to pick truth. What do you want to know?"

"If you'd had to explain me to Pandora, what would you have said?"

"What do you think I'd have said?"

"That sometimes you like to fuck the help."

"Damn. That's harsh, but not wrong."

My guts twisted on themselves and my self-respect demanded I get up and leave. The rest of me refused to budge.

"Fuck all, that's not what I meant."

"I think it was."

"No, I just meant that I'd have dismissed this as being... I wouldn't have said... not like that."

"There's nothing wrong with being the help anyway," he reassured me.

"No, there's not." I huffed. "So like what? I really need an answer. I need to hear it out of your mouth. I've already put my own words in your mouth and played them over and over like a woodchipper to my self-respect. Let me have your words."

"I'd have told her that first, who I fuck is none of her business. And second, that like all the women I fuck, you mean nothing to me."

Now, I wouldn't ever forget.

You mean nothing to me.

Straight out of his mouth. Tattooed in the inside of my skull forever and ever. So if I should get a case of the stupid, I could close my eyes and read those words. I could replay them over and over like my favorite song.

You mean nothing to me.

"Thank you for telling me."

Incongruent to his words, he kissed the top of my head and held me close.

Fucker.

At least now, I wouldn't be wondering what he really meant. If he just needed to be loved to be able to love. I knew you couldn't fix people. You had to take them as they were, I'd just doubted who he really was.

He'd told me. Loud and clear.

When people tell you who they are, you have to believe them. Don't at your own peril.

Still, I stayed.

I slept in his arms because I didn't want to be anywhere else.

Dumbass.

When I awoke in the morning, he was already gone. I didn't expect anything else. Although, he did leave me a coffee and a Danish on the nightstand. With one of his shirts folded neatly.

I wasn't going to wear it.

That, of course, was a lie.

My first class that morning was statistics, and I wanted to hang myself. Instead, I just kept smelling his shirt. Even though it was clean, it still smelled like him.

I saw Barclay between classes and he asked, "Is that Hunt's shirt?"

"Uh, yeah. It is."

"Seems like the weekend brought you closer. My loss." He shrugged and smiled.

I grinned at him. "Do you still want to be friends?"

"Yeah. I'd like that."

"Me too." I was glad, because if he didn't, that meant he was probably a shitty person and my judge of character was extremely poor. Current situation notwithstanding.

"So our father—"

"Let's not talk about that. Hunt and I aren't dating. We're just—" *You don't matter to me.*

"—having fun." He finished the sentence for me. "Everything'll work itself out, you know."

"One way or another."

He nodded. "The weekend brought Hunt and I closer, too."

"I'm really glad to hear it." I didn't understand how, but they could both use some real family. Everyone at this fucked up place could.

"Hey, are you busy? Want to grab a coffee?"

"I'm actually headed to Western Civ. But I could go after." Honestly, I didn't want to go back to the pod. Not yet.

"Great. I'll meet you at Black Dog?"

"Sure."

I wondered at my own motives for agreeing to meet Barclay. Kissing him had been nice. Hanging out with him had been nice. I'd have still been daydreaming about him, if not for Dane.

I realized I hadn't been thinking of him as Dane, but as Hunt.

Oh, that was bad.

Before him, though, I'd have been so happy with the turn of events with Barclay. If only.

Maybe it was just my contrarian nature and Hu—Dane's, too, that made this so delicious. We just wanted what we couldn't have. The more we denied ourselves, the more we wanted it.

Although, we'd given in to every single dirty desire that night we'd spent together and that didn't stop either of us from wanting more.

Good sex does not a good relationship make, I reminded myself.

All through Western Civ, I let myself think about what actually being with Hunt would be like. I let my mind wander. Not just thinking about the immediate where we'd fuck like rabid bunnies on Viagra.

But the really real reality of what a future with him would be like.

I imagined we'd end up just like my parents and his.

I shuddered. It was a horrible thought and it was the kind of life I knew for sure I didn't want.

When the passion ebbed. When we were done with each other, we'd be shackled in hell. I had no doubt this passion would last us long enough to flip our middle fingers to the world and we'd do the big wedding. The honeymoon on the Riviera. We'd buy a McMansion in the suburbs, but we'd keep apartments in the city. Weekend at one of the lakes. We'd both end up "working late" night after night. That's not to say it would start that way. Or either of us would intend it to be like that.

But no doubt it would. We'd both be chasing someone who made us feel something because we'd rip it out of each other. I get tired of getting hurt and he'd say he knew his father had been right all along.

We wouldn't get divorced, of course. We'd stay together. Unless he ran away with his secretary.

But I didn't plan on being some society wife. I would have my own business. My own money. My own protections.

That didn't make a future with him any more palatable.

Except then my brain wandered into more dangerous territory. What if it didn't have to be that way?

Oh, you silly summer child.

Yet, what if? What if we did fall in love. What if those long nights working late were spent working together? What if we built our own company from the ground up and actually did waive our middle fingers at everyone and everything? What if it was Hunt and I against the world, and we won?

I knew the likelihood of that was exactly zero.

And it did hurt to dream.

It hurt so much.

I had put it and him out of my head. Maybe as soon as I was able, I'd find someone else to sleep with. Shae would say the best way to get over one man was to get under another. I didn't know if I agreed with that, but it couldn't hurt to try.

Although, it wouldn't be Barclay.

I didn't want to do anything to damage their chances to rebuild their relationship. Although, that might be the thing he couldn't forgive.

That was why he'd tried to set me up with him in the first place.

Part of me wanted to run. To just move out of Ridgemont Hall all together and then I wouldn't have to think about him or see him. Unless I went to another of these stupid parties.

Although, it wasn't so stupid.

I'd really gotten to know Shae, made friends with Lauren, and Bastian. Those friendships meant something to me.

And hiding, as good as that sounded in the moment, wasn't going to solve anything. It's not like I could hide from myself.

That was really the problem. Not Hunt, or The Twosome of Gruesome. Just me.

I was still lost in my own thoughts when I realized everyone was leaving the lecture hall and I'd basically been checked out for the entire class.

Get your shit together, Asher. Or you're going to be a Cinder Girl.

I walked over to The Black Dog where Barclay was waiting for me.

"Latte?"

"God, yes. Thank you."

We sat down at a table in the corner and we sipped our coffees for a few minutes in comfortable silence before he spoke.

"Lauren liked you a lot."

"I liked her too. You guys should think about dating again."

"No, not a chance. We'd drive each other crazy."

"Isn't that the point? Pick the person you want to harass for the rest of your life?"

"Maybe that's how you and Hunt do things, but I want something a bit more relaxed."

"No, you don't. You think you do, but you don't. You have all the perks of dating with none of the work. How long before she gets tired of that and lets herself fall in love with someone else?"

"That would imply that she's in love with me now."

"She is, dumbass."

He looked like a deer frozen on the tracks in front of an oncoming freight train. "No, we've had this discussion."

"Maybe she doesn't know it herself, but she does."

"So when are you going to tell my brother that you're in love with him?"

I didn't miss a beat. "When shit sticks to the moon and tastes like apple butter."

"In this scenario, who is going to test the shit to see what it tastes like?"

"That's the point, Barclay."

"So, then you'll be looking for someone to take your mind off of him."

He was shrewder than Hunt gave him credit for. "No. Not yet. Not until he starts sleeping with someone else. Then I'm going to have hurt feelings, even though I agreed to what we're doing now. That's passive-aggressive, isn't it? I should just be honest, but I'm too scared. Right now, I can still pretend. How's that?"

"If we were talking about anyone but my brother, I'd say you were a coward. But we're not. My family is fucked, not to put too fine a point on it. So I'd say you were treading water pretty well."

"That's the thing. I don't want a future of just treading water."

"And you think Hunt doesn't know that?"

"No. Don't do that. Don't tell me that deep down, he's really this or that. Or he feels this or that. You can't do that. I'll drive myself crazy. He has to be who he is. On the surface. To me. Otherwise, it doesn't matter."

"You're right. I'm sorry. I just don't want either of you to get hurt."

"How dumb is this? He'd originally brought me out to the house to set us up."

"I really think you should elaborate." He took another drink of his coffee. "I need to hear how this whole thing was hatched into existence."

"It's dumb. It's really dumb. I had this list labeled Boyfriend Material that he snatched from me. He made fun of me for days, but then he got serious. He asked me what I really wanted and he swore he could help me get any man I wanted."

"And you wanted me?"

"Well, yes. I'd been crushing on you for years. Don't let that go to your head."

"This gets better and better."

"He didn't tell me you were brothers until he dropped it on me like a bomb at the house. He did, however, say he didn't think we'd be a good fit because I could tell you that a thesaurus was a newly discovered dinosaur."

"I'm no Rhodes Scholar, but I'm not that stupid."

"He was right though." I bit my lip. "Shit, not like that."

I remembered Hunt's words again from last night. Gah, I wished my brain would just shut up. I needed to switch channels from Hunt TV to anything else. Cross country Hungarian Poodle Grooming. Anything.

"Just that we're not a good match. You're great, hot as all hell, but there's no real fire."

"You're right. And I think you like arguing."

"I might."

"You should consider law."

"Too expensive and too much school. I want to get started being a shark sooner rather than later. My portfolio needs me."

We laughed.

"See, you're more like Hunt than you thought."

"I know. It's terrible, isn't it?"

"Basically," he agreed. "So why aren't you rushing back to his room?"

"Actually, I really want to talk about something that isn't him. How about Lauren and why I think you should date?"

"Didn't we cover that?" Barclay narrowed his eyes at me.

"Not to my satisfaction."

"I'm going to nix that topic."

"What's left?"

"Shae and Bastian?" he offered.

"Good one. They should totally date."

"How can we make this happen?"

"Oh, a project? We can get Lauren in on this."

"I thought you didn't want to talk about Lauren." I turned the subject neatly back to where I wanted it.

He narrowed his eyes again. See, it was a good thing we didn't hook up. I was pretty sure I'd make him do that all the time and he'd be wearing a permanent scowl.

"I don't. But she can help. She's really good at this kind of thing and with as anti-Bastian as Shae is and anti-relationship as Bastian is, we need reinforcements."

"I accept your logic this time, but be aware, I am going to call you on your shit from here on out."

"I expect no less, but you should know, I'm not the only one with 'shit.'"

I laughed. "Yeah, we all poop, Barclay. Didn't your mom read that book to you when you were little?"

"No, she didn't actually."

"You were robbed."

"In more ways than one."

DANE

I'D THOUGHT I was going to The Black Dog to grab an espresso. Or four.

But I saw her there with Barclay.

They were laughing. Smiling. Her posture was relaxed and she was at ease with him in a way I'd never seen her around me.

Instant, white-hot, stabbing jealousy arced through me.

I shut it down.

It was a useless expenditure of energy and emotion that would lead nowhere that either of us wanted to be.

It wasn't like we were dating. We'd both agreed that was a terrible proposition. What would that get us anyway?

A few years of us swearing we weren't going to be our parents and then what? Becoming them anyway?

I shuddered.

There would be nothing worse than living that life.

Nothing.

Even though I was halfway there, wasn't I?

I didn't know if it made it better or worse that I could actually see the slippery slope as I started to roll down it.

Fuck.

I went back to the pod. I kept thinking about her there with Barclay. I knew, somehow, that nothing was going to happen between them. Not like that, but I wanted her time and attention. I wanted to be the one out for coffee with her.

Shit.

Fuck.

SoddingBloodyMuppetFuck.

I slammed the door when I got inside, the cabinet when I got a bowl for my Weetabix, the refrigerator when I got the milk and Pandora opened her door.

"What is your problem? Some of us are trying to sleep?"

"It's three o'clock in the afternoon, Pandora. Why are you still sleeping? Oh. Nevermind." I took a bite of my Weetabix and thoroughly enjoyed the crunch.

"Are you going to answer me?"

"No," I said after I'd swallowed my bite. I was about to shove another in my mouth when Pandy put her hand on mine.

"Oh dear. Tell me you're not angsting over the cinder girl."

"No."

"Yes, you are. Fine. Tell Pandy all about it."

"Definitely not."

"I can't help you with your sins until you admit them."

"It's not a sin."

"Oh, this is worth than we thought."

"I'm not in the mood for this, Pandora."

"Who is? I mean, confession is bad for the likes of us."

I considered unburdening myself, but I'd sooner chew razor blades and gargle with salt water. It would hurt less in the long run.

"I'm fine. Just miffed. I'm sorry I disturbed your beauty rest." I inspected her. "Those bags are a little dark. You should go back to bed. Have a cucumber mask or something. Drink some lemon water."

She gasped. "You're mean."

"What is it you always say? A real friend is honest. I don't want you running around with Vuitton luggage under your eyes, love."

"True, true. Come sit with me while I hydrate and tell me. I really do want to help."

"I know you do. I'll figure it out."

"Okay, but darkling, promise me no more slamming."

"Turn on your white noise. Just in case."

"Too right. Too right." She went back to her room.

I proceeded to eat the whole box. Not my finest moment, but I was just crunching and crunching and the whole box was gone.

Now I was irritated I'd eaten all my Weetabix.

She'd left her door open.

Asher, not Pandora. Pandora was locked tight like a vampire in a coffin.

It'd be creepy of me to go in there, right? Like, lie down on the bed and wait for her? It would be a violation. A trespass.

Except I hadn't gotten my other shirt back from her. I was going to do laundry. Who was I kidding? I was going to send it out.

But she wouldn't mind if I went in and got it.

No, no. Bad idea.

I went in my own room and sat down on the bed. Maybe I should've waited for her to get up this morning. Or I should've woke her before I left. So I wouldn't be waiting for her to happen.

That's what I was doing.

I wanted this first post-apocalypse world encounter to hurry up and happen so I could be done with it.

I waited all day.

Until she finally came back to the pod. She slammed the door when she came in too. And the door to the refrigerator.

"For fuck's sake, not you too." Pandora opened her door. "He was all Slammy McFuckfacerson today too. You should just date so you can take your frustration out on each other. Instead of us."

"Jesus, Pandora. You look like shit."

"That's not going to work. He said that too."

"Really. You're all inflamed. You should go take a nap and *not* drink tonight."

"Since when do you care about what I do?"

"Since I've never seen you so tired."

Pandora gasped and shut the door.

"Shit, if I'd known that's all it takes I'd have tried it years ago," she muttered to herself.

Except Pandora opened the door again. "One more thing. If you two assholes don't date, you should at least keep fucking him. I can't take that nap you both so desperately wish I would take with all this noise!" she shrieked and slammed the door again.

"I see you," Asher said.

I smirked to myself, but I didn't open the door.

"You should come out."

"Or maybe you should come in?" I eased the door open a crack.

"I don't know. I don't think I should."

"Fine. I'll come to your room." She yelped when I threw her over my shoulder and hauled her into her room. We flopped on her very small twin bed.

"You didn't say raincheck."

"Nope. Because I think we should actually talk."

"I don't wanna."

"Yeah, me either."

"Oh, this must be bad. Okay. Lay it on me," she said.

"I was thinking today. About you. About us."

"Oh really? I was too."

Maybe best to let her go first. "What did you think?" I asked.

"Hell no. You first."

"Fine." I rolled my eyes. "I thought about how much I didn't want this to end. How I wanted to see you. Be close to you. Then I thought about what that would be like. It's a future I don't want."

"Nice. Shithead." She snorted.

"Come on. Don't tell me you didn't really think about us. Together. If you didn't, I'm going to feel so stupid. So stupid, I'll be praying for an aneurysm to rupture and end this. Or maybe a comet. A giant solar flare. Something."

She laughed. "God, no. Me too. I did. I thought about how right now it would be good. I think we'd have a good time. We have similar desires. Barclay told me that you and I are actually a lot alike. Which is slightly terrifying."

"Yeah. But eventually, we'd be our parents. I don't want that."

"Me either."

"So maybe we shouldn't raincheck either."

She exhaled heavily. "I thought about that too, and I don't want to stop. But maybe that's why we should. Before it gets ugly. Before we hate each other again."

"I still hate you. I hate you so much," I said, but I kissed that spot on her neck she liked.

"Hate me some more." She tangled herself around me. "No, no. Wait. It's my turn to hate you."

She pushed me onto my back and took after my trousers with her teeth.

Oh, Christ.

My hands were in her hair and her mouth was bliss made of hellfire on my skin. She took my cock in her mouth and I was still sore, but it didn't matter. Only being with her did. Only touching her.

No one had ever done this for me like this. Just for my pleasure. Because she wanted to. So many lovers had done it because they thought they were supposed to. They thought that was the way to make me care.

It wasn't.

Those other times had still brought me off, but not like this. Not like her.

"This is going to be over so very fast if you keep that up."

She looked up at me and smiled. "Good. Why don't you look at this like a competition? I'm going to try so hard to make you come and you're going to fight it."

She pushed all of my buttons at once. She made it a battle and I knew I was going to lose.

I didn't care.

I only cared about this moment with her.

She worked my cock with a singular abandon. I did my best to fight her. To think about something else, anything else while she took me deep again and again.

I failed miserably.

I've never been so happy to fail.

"I'm going to come," I warned her. As was polite.

"I know. Give it to me."

The orgasm washed over me in waves as I spilled into her mouth. She took it all and I knew I'd be thinking about that the next time I wanked. She licked every last drop and then she kissed me full on the mouth.

"Good, I'm glad you're not one of those who won't kiss his girl after she blows him. That's rude."

"Are you my girl? My Cinder Girl?"

"I am."

I was about to return the favor when a loud knock sounded on her door. "Sod off, we're busy."

She giggled.

The knock sounded again, this time more forceful. "Listen, mate, I said we're busy and I don't like repeating myself when my mouth's full. It's fucking rude."

"It is, but your father would like an audience," my father said.

Oh fucking fuck of all fucks.

There weren't enough fucks to fuck.

"I'm in the middle of something, so if you'll be so kind as to give me a moment," I said, pulling on my mask of indifference.

She bit her lip and put her hand on my face. "It's okay."

"No, it's really not." I mouthed. "Wait here."

She nodded and I righted myself.

It was a sad case I was supposed to be a grown man but still lived in fear of my father like he was some kind of brutal warlord. Maybe he was, but modern standards. What was the worst he could do to me? Take away my birthday? My inheritance?

No. The worst thing he could do to me was take away his affection. His esteem.

My worth as his heir.

He'd already made it clear he had affection for Barclay, but Barclay wasn't the one whom he'd taken out kidnapping insurance. Barclay didn't have a trust. He had a black card, but those funds were dependent on my father's goodwill. My trust was mine when I turned thirty no matter what. These were the ways my father showed his love.

And I'd seen them taken away. Like what he did to Barclay's

mother. Abandoning her when she was pregnant. He didn't take care of his responsibility until a court forced him to.

I steadied myself and went out to face him.

He was sitting at the table in the kitchen. Looking completely out of place. It was like one of those paintings for children to find the thing that didn't belong.

My father.

I often wondered if I came across the same way. I probably did.

"If you'd let me know you were coming—"

"You'd have hidden your low rent whore?"

"She's not a whore. I haven't paid her a dime."

"She's just like her mother."

"And I'm just like my father. What does it matter?"

"No. You're not like me at all. I didn't date Barclay's mother. I didn't marry her. I never let anyone see me in public with her. I've heard you've been very public with your indiscretion with this girl. What happened to introducing her to Barclay?"

"Contrary to your belief, people do make decisions based on their on their own needs. Their own wants. They may be in opposition to yours."

"No. Have you learned nothing? You make it in their best interest to do what you want. Whatever that takes."

"What about what I want?"

He laughed and the sound was cold and empty. "You're not old enough to know what you want."

"I know enough that I don't want to be you."

He went still and I knew that meant he was about to strike. "I thought you could be better than me, but I see now you got the weaker genes. End it with her."

"No."

"End it with her or I'll stop payment on the check for your tuition."

"No."

"End it with her or I'll stop payment on Barclay's tuition."

"What do I care? You always told me he's not really my brother. That he's just a contender for my crown," I spat.

"I'll cut your mother off."

"Good luck. She'd have you in court so fast your head would literally spin around on your neck."

"I've taught you well, but I still have the power here. You know why? I'll have the committee revoke her scholarship."

"I guess that's up to her, then. Isn't it?"

"You don't really think she'll pick you over paid tuition and a hundred thousand dollars in her bank account free and clear, do you?"

If I was in her position, I know I wouldn't. That was a game changer. I'd pick the money over me any day. She was shrewd, but I didn't think she could live with picking money over her humanity. That's how she'd see it. She wouldn't do it.

Even if she didn't really want me. She'd dig in her heels just to prove she couldn't be bought.

I wouldn't let her do that. She could have the future she wanted.

All I had to do was stop being a selfish bastard and let go.

I could protect myself from him, but I couldn't protect her. Neither of us were dragons. We both still needed saving.

And in that equation, we'd both drown.

"No," she said from the door.

"I see you've been utilizing your selective listening skills," I drawled, doing my best to act like none of this mattered to me. "I told you to wait."

"And I'm not going to let some old man decide my future. Revoke my scholarship. I don't care." She threw her phone done. "I recorded everything you said. Maybe I won't find a judge who'll side with me, but I'll release it to the media. Somewhere, I'll find someone who'll fight you. I'm not afraid of you."

"You should be. Ten years from now, when you still don't have a job in finance because I've closed all those doors for you, you'll wish you'd taken the money."

"Ten years from now, when I own everything you used to, you'll roll over in your grave," she said quietly.

Her mouth had just written a check her ass was not yet ready to cash.

My father took threats very seriously.

"None of this is necessary," I said, while my heart shattered in my chest. I pushed the pieces down to the dark place inside where I couldn't see it, hear it, or worst of all, feel it. "Don't throw away your future on a good orgasm. That's all this was."

I saw the line of her mouth go thin, the set to her jaw harden even more. Her back straightened and her shoulders squared. She was gearing up for another fight. Until I looked in her eyes and saw the fight was with herself and not me.

It fucking killed me to see it.

It killed me to do it.

I'd mourn what I'd broken. What I'd thrown away.

She'd never forgive me for this, and I didn't blame her. Right now, I should've backed her play. Stood my ground, if that's what she wanted. But this was her future. I loved her too much to let her throw it away.

I loved her too much to let us slide down this slope into the lives of our parents.

I'd always remember her as my almost.

I'd always remember her as the one I did love more than myself.

And goddamn it, I'd also remember the way she looked at me right now. The words I said and how they were like knives for us both.

"Little Cinder Girls play in the ashes and sometimes they get a fairy godmother. Yours came, just not like you thought."

He squeezed my shoulder. "Good choice, son. Yet, your bit of rebellion was welcome. You'll stand your ground for something you really want. Obviously, this wasn't it. Which is also welcome knowledge. I'll have that account set up today."

I didn't look at her again.

"Good. See that you do. Have the appropriate documents messengered over. I'd like proof."

"Of course. I'll see you Thanksgiving?"

"I was thinking of going to Monte Carlo," I said, making sure to keep my tone neutral. I didn't ever want to look at his face again.

"So was your mother. I'll get our regular suites."

I could feel her rage, her pain, and all the words she'd left unsaid hanging over my head like the Sword of Damocles.

125

The words I wanted to say to her hung there too, heavy with regret.

Yet, in the end, I said nothing.

I went to my room and closed the door. The lock clicking into place echoed like the report of a shotgun.

ASHER

THAT...

I didn't have a word strong enough to call him at the moment.

I knew his father was a First Class Fucko. Hunt didn't have to be. But he was. He didn't have the faith in me that I could stand up to him.

Well, fuck them both.

In the eye.

With a syphilitic bag of dicks.

I wasn't going to let this break me.

Except I was crying. He'd thrown me away without a second thought. No wait, that was wrong. He'd had a single moment where he believed. It was the second thought that did him in.

Did *us* in.

But what did I expect, really? We knew this was coming. It was only a matter of when. He'd get bored. I'd get bored. Or something better would come along.

He made the choice for both of us.

I guess I shouldn't be pissed at him that he tried to protect me. I know that was part of it, but really, he wanted to protect himself.

I couldn't blame him.

Correction. I *shouldn't* blame him. But I did.

I was standing there, in a pair of joggers and a cami, crying over the inevitable. It startled the fuck out of me when Conrad came out of his room, saw me crying, and instead of minding his own business, he put his arm around me.

"Oh, Asher."

He made me a cup of hot chocolate, while I stood there like a dumb animal waiting to be led to slaughter. He took another look at me and spiked the hot chocolate with whiskey.

He took a swig himself, and then added another shot. "Here you go."

Conrad handed me the warm cup and led me to his room. Again, like a dumb animal, I followed.

"Do all evil minions have alcoholic hot chocolate making skills?"

"Minion?" he snorted. "It's special order."

"I figured." I couldn't stop crying. At least I hadn't started the full-on sobbing yet, but I didn't have long. "So, I appreciate this, but I'm about to cry ugly."

"I know. H2 is a shitheel of the lowest caliber."

"H2?"

"Easier than Huntington Dane the II. H2. Not as impressive as H3, if we're being honest."

"Yeah, well H3 is being a fucko, too."

"I couldn't help but hear everything that went down, of course."

"Of course." I sniffed and he handed me a monogrammed kerchief that I would've felt terrible using until he glared at me. "Nothing worse than a sniffling anyone."

"Isn't that a line from a movie?"

"Perhaps about sniffling women, but really, it's not attractive on anyone."

I took a fortifying drink of the hot chocolate and it warmed me all the way down.

"Anyway," Conrad said. "I heard what he did. He basically gave you a future. You can't be upset with him for that."

"I'm not upset about that. I'm upset that he didn't trust me to choose."

"Of course not. You'd have chosen him, wouldn't you?"

"Yes. And it's my choice to make." Frustration knotted inside me.

"Did you ever think maybe he didn't want that pressure?"

"What do you mean?" I tried not to sniff again.

"Imagine if he gave up his education for you. How would that make you feel?"

I wanted to say I would trust him to make his own choices, but I wouldn't. I wouldn't want him to hate me for it. Whether the relationship led to some kind of future or not.

It was like turning on a light.

I understood.

"That doesn't mean I have to like it."

"I'm sure he doesn't either."

"How did his father even know?"

"He's probably paying Pandy to spy on him."

"I guess she gets her Fucko rank, too. Sergeant. Second Class. What about you? Are you on the payroll?"

"I was, but I didn't tattle on you. I was too busy trying to make sure Pandora didn't eat me."

"I think you were supposed to eat her." I snickered, amused at my own double entendre.

"Yeah, that's the problem. I've seen what she does to men. How she snares them in her trap. Hell, I've helped her devise some truly wicked schemes using her body. No way would I go into the spider's web willingly."

"Yet, you did."

"It was the key party. I didn't have a choice."

"So you were forced?"

"Yes. Basically. Coerced." He nodded. "Yes."

I raised an eyebrow.

"What? I'd be out of the club if I didn't go upstairs with her. She even said so. After she said she didn't particularly want to have sex with me, and called me a little bitch to boot."

"You still didn't have to do it."

"You know better than that."

"So now what?"

"That's the problem. Pandy and I have always been... not that. In fact, I'm pretty sure she didn't even know I had a penis until last night."

"Neither did I, to be fair."

"Do you want your fucko stripes too, because I just made you hot chocolate."

I sniffed.

"And gave you a nice kerchief to grieve and snot upon."

"I know. I'm sorry."

"Good. You should be. So here are our options: Be sad. Hide. Fuck someone else. Or each other."

"That would be great revenge, but I just don't know if we can."

"We could try. It would really stick in Pandora's craw."

"Sideways? Like that much?"

"Definitely that much."

"I don't know that Hunt will care, and if he does, I don't want to hurt him more than he's already hurting."

"Oh please. He made his choice, didn't he? He made yours too. This one is all yours, babe."

Babe? "Are you even attracted to me? I mean..."

"Of course. Why else do you think Pandy hates you? It's not because of your dad. That just made you an easier mark. Pandy has hated you since your eighth birthday party when you didn't invite her."

"Holy balls, I didn't even make that list myself. Are you serious?"

"Usually."

I took another drink of the hot chocolate. "Wait, are you trying to get me drunk so you can seduce me?"

"No. I was trying to get you drunk so you spent enough time in here with me that Pandy would think we had sex. Hunt, too. Just because."

"You're a horrible human being."

"True."

I wanted to find him attractive and I could say he fit the classic standard of beauty, but he wasn't Hunt. I found I had a sudden affinity for icy blonds, just damn my luck.

The idea of sleeping with him just to piss off Pandora and make Hunt think about what he'd thrown away was appealing, and in some other time and place, I might have done it.

Stupid me didn't want anyone but Hunt.

"What is it the kids say? Get over one man by getting under another?"

"Probably not, Conrad."

"Too bad."

"I know. It's a great revenge plot. I can't say it won't have its appeal after I'm done hurting and I move on to being angry."

"Well, I'm just a knock away. If Pandora hasn't devoured me like a Black Widow Spider yet."

"Or maybe like those fish. What are they called? They're those really ugly deep sea bastards where the male just sort of merges with the females body?" I added.

"Thanks. That was helpful."

"I try." I took a sip of my hot chocolate. "This is really good. Thank you."

"Any time, Cinder."

The name didn't hurt me anymore. At least, not in the way it used to.

"You know, you should really give Pandora a dose of her own medicine."

"Well, I was trying, but you said no." His mouth was pressed into a thin line.

"It doesn't have to be me, but what would she do if you pursued her. Like, actually pursued her. I bet she'd run like prey."

"You think?"

"You know what you're feeling right now? All turned around and fucked up? Don't you think if you were the aggressor, she'd feel exactly the same way."

"Or she'd bite my head off and save my body to feed her young."

"Maybe. Or maybe you'd both get what you want."

"You're evil, Asher. I quite like that about you. It's a subtle evil. It hides under your skin."

"Thank you?"

A furious knock sounded at the door. "Conrad," Pandora demanded.

"Busy, doll."

"Did I hear Asher in there with you?"

"Mmm, you did. Poor thing is quite tense. I'm making use of my massage and cocktail skills, since you didn't need me."

"I need you now."

"Busy now."

"What, is Asher our friend now? No. I didn't agree to this."

"Too bad."

"Oh," I cried out. "That's just the spot. Harder, Conrad. Mmhmm."

"Nicely played," he whispered.

"Thanks."

I heard her door slam. Then I heard another slam across the hall. It had to be Hunt.

And to my shame, I started crying again.

"I thought we were done with that? No?"

I blubbered.

"Gross. Fine. I don't think I'm equipped for this. Can I call someone for you?"

"Shae."

Conrad pulled out his phone and dialed a number. "No, I didn't expect to be calling you either, but I think we have an emergency."

"Wait," I sniffed. "Why do you have Shae's number?"

"I'll let her explain."

I guess I wasn't the only one who'd taken a walk on the fucko side.

"No," he said back into the phone. "Come get her. She's a mess. Yes, now." He hung up. "She's on her way."

I thought that maybe I should've called Barclay, but I realized that while I had the power to say no to Conrad, Barclay would be another story. He'd be kind. He'd be understanding. He'd be safe.

And he'd be the blade in Hunt's back.

The kerchief he'd given me was... full. I was so grossed out. "I'll wash it and give it back."

He waved it off. "No, don't. Really. My gift."

I sniffled again. "I'm sorry."

It wasn't long before there was a knock on the pod door and Conrad shuffled me out of his room and toward the door.

Shae took one look at me and said, "Oh, let's get you the hell out of here. Come on. We're going back to my place."

"Please tell me why Conrad had your number?"

"Chemistry."

"The class or..."

"Eh, both. Mistakes were made in the bloom of my youth." She laughed. "It doesn't matter. Maybe he had it in his phone for just this moment. The universe is looking out for you, kid."

"Doubt."

"Stop that. This sucks right now, and you're going to tell me all about why it sucks, and I'm going to listen carefully. I'll tell you why it doesn't, and we're going to have ice cream, champagne, and if you want me to kill someone for you, we'll go buy a tarp. Okay?"

I laughed. "Okay."

Except I didn't talk. I rode all the way to her apartment off campus in silence. I didn't know where to start. Should it have been with, *well, I'm a dumbass who...* or, *against all judgment I let myself have feelings for...* or... I could just start with:

"He threw me away."

"Oh, honey. Tell me what happened." Shae put her arm around me and I let myself lean on her shoulder.

I spewed out the whole sordid tale from the beginning to the bitter end. Up to and including Conrad's suggestion.

"You know, I'm on Team Conrad on this one. Sort of."

"What do you mean?"

"The point of being with someone else is remind *yourself* that you can be intimate with someone else. Not to pay him back. Not for revenge. It's to find your center. Your self-love. That's definitely not with Conrad. He's terrible in bed anyway."

"Oh god." I found myself laugh-crying. "Boy, I'm fucked up. I can't decide if I'm laughing or crying."

"It's both, and that's okay."

"Like, how bad in bed? Did I dodge a bullet?"

"You didn't dodge anything. He couldn't find a clitoris with a map and both hands."

We snorted and laughed because we snorted, then laughed at the idea of Conrad in spelunking gear looking for the mythical clitoris.

"Don't let anything that happened tonight make you doubt yourself. If you don't right now, tomorrow or the next day or whenever you decide to dissect it, you're going to doubt every choice you made along the way. Don't do that."

"I do that constantly. How do I stop?"

"You remember that you hold your power. No one can take that from you. All you can control are your own actions. You did everything the way you thought was best. At the time, it probably was."

"Even falling into bed with Huntington Dane?"

"Yes, even that. All of your wins make you who you are, but so do your falls. Especially your falls. When you skin your knee ugly, it changes you forever. It leaves a scar. But that skin is tougher than it was before. You will be too. Just don't forget to get back up."

"You're like a self-help guru or something."

"Eh, I just went through some shit and came out the other side. It happens to all of us."

She was right about that.

"I wish I could make this better for you, but I can't. So I'll just be here with you while you make it better for yourself."

"Thanks for believing that I can."

"Of course you can. You can do anything, Asher. If anyone tells you differently, I'm going to get that tarp."

"You don't think I should run out and bang Barclay?"

"Do you think that's going to bring you resolution or peace?"

"No. But it might be nice for now."

"It might. Or you could wait for that pizza I ordered while you were crying and crawl in bed with me and we can watch John Hughes movies."

"That sounds better. Everything works out in the end, even for the shitty people. Except Stef in *Pretty in Pink*. God, his hair was pretty." I sighed. "Hunt's a Stef, isn't he?"

"He might be a Blaine." She shrugged. "I guess time will tell."

She gave me a face masque and pair of fuzzy slippers and we crawled into her bed. She put her arm around me and stroked my hair and told me it was all going to be okay.

For that moment, I believed her.

DANE

I DIDN'T KNOW what else to do.

Except I knew what I had done was the right thing. I wasn't going to let her throw away her future, the chance to beat everyone who'd tried to break her for me.

I hadn't seen her in a week, and I knew that was for the best, too.

I avoided The Black Dog. I avoided the pod. I avoided Conrad. I avoided Barclay. I avoided everyone and everything that wasn't on my immediate needs list.

Basically, I went to class and I stayed at a hotel.

I just couldn't bring myself to go anywhere I might see her. I know, giant coward. But I was okay with that. Anything to avoid seeing her and the condemnation and betrayal in her eyes.

She'd never forgive me, and maybe someday, I'd be in her sites to take down and destroy.

Bloody hell, but that gave me a hard-on.

What was actually wrong with me? I didn't know, but I should probably figure it out.

I got a text from Barclay.

Bastard Brother: *Truth or Dare. Friday night. Common Area.*

I didn't reply.

Bastard Brother: *I know you saw that. You're coming, right?*

Me: *NO.*

Bastard Brother: *Yes, you are.*

Me: *Asher and I are done.*

Bastard Brother: *So that means you don't want to play your favorite game? You're either not actually Hunt, or you're sick. Which is it?*

Me:... *fuck off.*

Bastard Brother: *I'm coming over.*

Me: *Not home.*

Bastard Brother: *Fine. Meet me.*

Me: *I'd rather gouge out my eyes with a melon baller.*

Bastard Brother: *You can do that after.*

Me: *Fine. Where?*

Me: *Also, you bring the melon baller.*

Bastard Brother: *Also fine. I'm at The Black Dog.*

Me: *Not happening.*

Bastard Brother: *For fuck's sake. Where then?*

Me: *Your mom's.*

Bastard Brother: *Fuck you. Be serious.*

Me: *The Brit.*

Bastard Brother: *Tea? Okay. Be there in twenty. You better be, too.*

Me: *I said I would.*

Bastard Brother: *No, you didn't. You said to go there. You didn't technically say you were coming. I know you.*

Me: *Yes, well, this is serious.*

The Brit was a lovely little shop that dealt in imported food items from the UK. It was the only place to get a decent cup of tea. Mostly, I drank coffee, but when things were serious, nothing could top a good cup of tea.

Except a good scotch, but getting pissed wasn't going to solve anything. It wouldn't even make me feel better.

The biscuits were slightly dry, but they reminded me of my childhood and my favorite nanny. I could also pick up another box of Weetabix. Or two.

One of the best parts of a cup of tea was the ritual. When I got to The Brit, I found they were out loose leaf Yorkshire Gold, but at least it wasn't bagged Twinnings. Only loose leaf, thank you very much.

I was surprised Barclay was coming. No, maybe I wanted to be surprised. He'd always been game for anything I'd ever told him to do now that I thought about it. I should probably try to be a better big brother, I mean, since we'd decided to try this brothers thing.

After all, he was saddled with the wanker who sired us, too.

Briefly, I thought about all the ways I could use that against him, like I'd been taught.

But I didn't want to be that person.

I never did.

Except, it became clear to me that I didn't have to be.

I could protect myself from my father and those like him without sacrificing what I wanted for myself.

Huh.

That was a revelation.

It was what Asher and Barclay had been trying to tell me all along.

Although, I still had to worry about those who got close to me. Like what he'd done to Asher. And by proxy, to me.

I was going to make him pay for what he'd done. I wasn't sure how yet. But I would. He had to learn that not every living thing could be a chess piece moved about on the board at his pleasure.

Sometimes, those pieces would go where they wished and there wasn't a sodding thing he could do about it.

Some of them even pushed back.

It wasn't long before Barclay came through the door and joined me at my table.

"Okay. Let's have it."

When I handed him the cup of tea, he said, "Yes, very nice. I mean about what happened."

I studied him for a long moment before I answered. I had been debating how much to tell him about what had happened. Whether it was okay to give him all of this ammunition.

That kind of thinking was second nature. I had to choose to let him in. I had to choose to trust him.

"Father threatened Asher."

"How did that go for him?" Barclay seemed to think that I'd somehow ridden to her rescue. That I'd saved her from the dragon. I guess I had, but not in the way he thought.

"He got his way, Barclay. What did you think would happen? He threatened to have her expelled and to pull her scholarship."

"He what? Why would he do that?"

"Because she's unacceptable as a partner for his heir."

"He just went for the throat."

"Not initially. He threatened your inheritance. Mine. My mother's credit line... It wasn't until he threatened Asher directly that I caved. And the fucker said he was glad to see I had a backbone."

Barclay shook his head. "What a fucker. So you and Asher are just done?"

"There's no other way to protect her."

"Don't you think that was up to her?"

"No, I don't. Because she's a better person than I am. She would've chosen wrong."

Barclay laughed. "But it's still up to her to choose, isn't it? It's her life. She's allowed to make mistakes because their hers to make."

"Still no."

He laughed again. "Dude. Seriously. Loving someone means leaving their autonomy intact."

"That's the most disgusting thing I've ever heard." I scowled.

"Which part? The love or the autonomy?"

"Both. It's terrible. How are you supposed to love someone if they're free to fuck about and damage themselves? I can't have this. I just can't."

"You do love her."

"Obviously."

"Have you told her this?"

"Of course not. I'm not good for her. The way I have to live... no. She's going to get her degree here and she's going to do everything she dreamed of doing. Which doesn't include me."

"How do you know?"

"I was her worst nightmare up until Bear Lake." I held up my hand.

"And she was mine. She's the worst thing that could happen to me. And I'm the worst thing that could happen to her."

"Yet, you'd give up everything to protect her."

"Shut it, Barclay. It's self-preservation."

"Is it really?"

"You sound too much like me when you say it like that. Stop it."

"I'm Brit-ish and poncy, and I don't care about anything but myself. Except I do and if you make me admit it, I'll punish you." Barclay rolled his eyes. "Listen. Give her the choice. If you go talk to her—"

"If I go talk to her I'm the biggest knob on two feet. Not doing it. What I am doing is avoiding all things Asher and definitely all things Truth or Dare."

"Pandora will never let you live it down if you don't play. You know the rules."

"Fuck the rules. And fuck Pandora. This isn't Brewer Prep."

"You're right about that, but you should come."

"Why? Give me one good reason."

"To see the fallout of what you've done."

"The laugh is definitely on you, Barclay. One of the best things about Asher Warren is that she's unbreakable. I could rip her heart out and eat it with chips and she'd never let anyone see the scar. Least of all me."

"If you won't reach out for her with both hands, someone else will. In the meantime, how are we going to make our father pay?"

"I've actually considered telling my mother. It's low. It's cheap. And it'll make his life a living hell."

"That's not a bad idea."

"I know, if I want him to take me seriously, I need to kick him in the bottom line."

"I might be able to help with that. Did you hear about the Pollix deal?"

"I did." My eyes narrowed. "He's acquiring Pollix Technology."

"Did you hear that he's having an affair with Pollix's wife? You could blow this deal all to shit."

I debated if I actually wanted to blow it, or if I wanted to threaten him. I quickly decided that he wouldn't take me seriously until I not only showed him my teeth, but I took a bite out of him.

"How do you know he's sleeping with her?"

"My mother keeps a close eye on him in case he's ever late with his support payments. I've got pictures. They could make their way to your email today, if you want."

"I do want."

"Are you going to give them to your mother?"

"No. I'm going to send them to arrange a meeting with Pollix."

"Oh, shit. You know this could backfire in your face like a fart."

I shrugged. "Maybe. But it's time for Huntington Dane II to learn a lesson. If I fail spectacularly, then I fail. He can't do anything else to me. He's already taken away the only thing I ever really wanted for myself."

"You did that yourself."

"And we're never going to speak of it again."

"Are you sure that's what you want to do?" Barclay said. "It's okay to grieve what you lost, you know."

"I've had enough feelings for the day."

"Sometimes they haven't had enough of you."

"You sound like a self-help book."

"My mother read enough of them when I was a kid." He shrugged.

"I suppose that you do know a thesaurus isn't a dinosaur. Sorry about that, mate."

"Yeah, She-Who-Must-Not-Be-Mentioned told me you said that."

"You know, you're still mentioning her."

"Fine. She-Who-Doesn't-Actually-Exist-Because-It-Hurts-Your-Lumplings."

"Oh fuck off, Barclay."

"You first."

I sipped my tea. It didn't have the same effect it usually did. The idea of going up against my father made me slightly ill. I still wanted his love and attention, but it was unlikely I'd ever get it.

This move seemed like such a betrayal of him, yet it was simply implementing everything he'd ever taught me. Maybe screwing with his bottom line was cutting off my nose to spite my face as they said, but maybe it had to be done.

Again, I was thankful my trust was untouchable.

Of course, if it wasn't, that would make this mean more. I was aware that my risk to reward ratio wasn't some magnificent leap.

This wasn't a grand gesture for Asher.

It was for me. No matter what else I did, I had to crawl out of his shadow. It was time.

And for Asher.

I wasn't going to let anyone threaten her. Especially not him.

"The look on your face right now is the same one you wore whenever you'd try to get me in trouble. What are you thinking?"

"Nothing. Just waiting for that email. Then I'll set a meeting with Pollix."

"Uh, if he loses his ass on this, you gonna take care of me in my old age?" Barclay teased.

"You should marry Lauren. For her money of course." I smirked.

"You know, Asher said Lauren and I should date."

"See?"

"I notice that you conveniently didn't answer my question."

"Don't be a fuck boy. Of course, I will. And don't make me tell you that I love you or anything else like that."

"Okay, not out loud, but I want it in writing."

"Ah, so you're a Dane after all."

"Somewhere, yeah. I guess I am."

"You are." I didn't want to think about what that must mean to him. Or to me. As children, I told him he'd never be a Dane. That he'd never be part of our family, but he was. He was *my* family now. Together, we'd be stronger.

Maybe that's what our father had always feared. We wouldn't need him. Or his money.

I had a startling and grim flash of the future. My father was going to grow old and die alone. Not all the money in the world on its own could change that.

I'd been on way to becoming the same man. With the same future.

My problem was now that when I let myself think of the future, there was no future in which I wasn't with Asher.

That was the most fucked up fairytale I'd ever told myself. The one least likely to ever happen.

A fairy godmother was more likely to fall out of a tree and give me three wishes and magic shoes before Asher and I would end up together.

"Hunt, it's all going to work out. I know it is."

That was another fairytale that I desperately wanted to believe.

"Come to the game Friday."

"Still not doing it. I just can't."

"Asher is going to be there."

"I'm sure she is. Which is why I won't."

"I don't know. Maybe you'll feel differently after you talk to Pollix."

"Doubt."

"Can we go get a beer now?" Barclay wrinkled his nose.

"Might as well." Tea hadn't helped. Beer wouldn't either, but I could be miserable anywhere.

We left The Brit and went to a frat boy bar on the other side of town. As we were walking inside, he said, "Hey, Lauren's here."

I put in my time hanging with my brother, but I was out of there as soon as I could manage it.

I had phone calls to make and a little bit of hell to raise.

Instead of setting a meeting with Pollix, I was going to call his wife.

My father would know I'd beaten him, Asher would be safe, but I'd also have a favor from Miranda Pollix in my back pocket.

It was always better to make friends than enemies.

It took some work to get her private cell number, but it was nothing I couldn't afford.

It was late that night when I finally called her. I was alone in a hipster donut bar drinking a whiskey sour with nothing to lose.

"What can I do for you, Baby Dane?" Miranda's voice was throaty and low. She sounded like she'd just been fucked, or wanted to be.

"I have a problem and I think you can fix it."

"Oh really?" She laughed. "Why would I do that?"

"Because if you don't, it's going to be your problem."

"Oh, please. Tell me this isn't some *stay away from my daddy* bullshit, because little man, he's my daddy now."

"Foul and unnecessary."

"Good. So what is it that you want?"

"I want you to pull your shares from the deal with my father."

"Whyever would I do that?" She laughed again. "Wait, *why* do you want me to do that is the real question. It would make you a ton of money."

"Some things are more important than money."

"Don't tell me. Is it love?"

"Of course not. It's beating an old dog at an old game."

"Now, I'm interested. If it was because of that Warren girl, and yes, Huntington told me all about it, I was going to throw up."

I let myself slip into the man my father had tried to make of me. "That's disgusting as well. No, it's about not being outmaneuvered. The Warren girl as you call her will benefit, but only because it will kick my father in the knob."

"Interesting. Tell me more. Why didn't you go to my husband?"

"I suppose I could have and the thought did occur to me, but what do I get out of that? And the victims always shoot the messenger. I'd rather have a favor in my back pocket from Miranda Pollix. I think we all know you're the one with the power in that relationship."

"Flattery will get you everywhere, Baby Dane."

"Good. Here's what I want. Pull your vote from the deal. Give the Warren girl a gig where she can learn something, but don't keep her so busy she can't study. Pay her well. And tell my father you're doing it because you spoke with me."

She laughed again and it was obvious she was amused. "What do I get out of it besides your silence? Because I don't really need it. My husband likes his allowance and if he leaves me, our prenup is ironclad. And you want an additional favor? An IOU? This better be good."

"It is. You get to exert your dominance over my father. You get a future working relationship with me. I'm a small fish now, but I'm going to outgrow this pond, and so will Asher Warren. She's driven. Fearless. She's majoring in finance and if you were to teach her and whitewash her reputation, she'd be loyal to you."

"I already exert dominance over your father. But I'll think it over. I assume that you'll take this to my husband if I don't comply?"

"Not at all."

"But you have some other devious thing in mind? Tell. I want to weigh all my options fully."

I debated not telling her but decided why the hell not. "I'm afraid I'll have to go to my mother. Mostly she doesn't give a solitary shite what he does as long as she gets her stipend, but when I tell her he's threatening my future happiness, and then supply her with the ammo to break their prenup, well... it could get ugly."

"I see that it could. Riddle me this, Baby Dane. Is this your first move against your father?"

"My first *significant* move."

"Having a controlling and domineering father myself, I understand exactly where you're coming from. And I was getting bored with Vintage Dane. This will spice things up."

"You'll do as I've asked?"

"Yes, yes. Have your little Asher report to the Miranda Hotel on Tuesday after class."

"About that. We're not exactly speaking."

"Oh because you chose her education for her? I see. Text me her number. I'll have my assistant call her and offer her a paid internship with me. I trust that suits all of your requirements?"

"It does."

"I want something from you, Baby Dane."

I was hoping she'd stop calling me that. It was making my skin crawl. "What is that?"

"Call me when you're a shark. I might have a business proposition for you."

"I will."

"Was there anything else? I'm meeting your father for a late, late dinner."

"No."

"Then I'll speak to you in about five years. Take care, little fish."

The line went dead.

I felt like I was going to throw up. I'd just fucked my father's bottom line in the worst possible way.

I should probably call my mother and warn her he was going to be in a foul mood and looking for payback.

For myself, I probably should go to Bora Bora. Except he'd find me there. There was nothing to do now with what I'd done except live with it.

All of it.

Losing Asher included.

But I felt better for what I'd done. No matter what happened now, Asher would be safe until she was strong enough to defend herself.

I hadn't saved her, I'd just given her the time and space to save herself which was what she wanted all along.

ASHER

"I'm not playing Truth or Dare tonight," I said to Lauren, who was flopped on my bed.

"Why not? Come on. It was fun last time." She grinned at me. "Don't you want to kiss me again?"

"I can do that without playing Truth or Dare, can't I?"

"No." She winked at me.

"You're wretched."

"You've been hanging out with Hunt too long. *Wretched*. Who uses that word? Besides English majors?"

"Me."

"Obviously. Listen, I have it on good authority Hunt won't be there."

"I don't care if he's there or not." Lies. All lies.

"Yes, you do. It's okay that you do."

"No, it's really not. He threw me away. He didn't trust me."

"He didn't trust himself, honey. That's not you."

"Enough about me. I'll start harassing you about Barclay."

"That is not a subject that needs discussion. We're best friends."

"Who have a lot of sex."

149

"Only when... sometimes. So?" Lauren sniffed. "We can have casual sex and still be good friends."

"Yeah, you can, but..." There was something in the set to her shoulders. Something was wrong. "Here I've been going on and on about my bullshit, but you've got something on your chest. What is it?"

"I'm scared to say it out loud."

"Wanna write it down?"

"That's dumb."

Lauren was silent for a long moment.

"But I can't seem to open my mouth and get the words to come out. So maybe?"

I shoved a notebook at her and a pen.

She wrote something down and shoved it back at me. She covered her face with her hands.

I'm pregnant.

"Holy fuckballs, what?"

She just shook her head.

"Are you sure?"

She nodded.

"Okay, so how do you feel about that?"

"Thanks for not asking me what I'm going to do because I have no idea. I'm not ready for a child. I think Barclay will be a good father, when he's ready, but now is not the time for either of us."

"You haven't said anything to him, have you?"

"Of course not. He's trying to make huge life decisions now. The NFL thing or staying in school. If I told him I was pregnant, he'd want to get married. Start a family and he'd choose the money option. Even though he gets money from his dad." Lauren pulled her knees up to her chest and wrapped her arms around them. "And even though he doesn't love me that way."

"I think he does. Honestly, I think you both have feelings you're not acknowledging for fear of change. Of losing the friendship you have. But I'm not one to be giving advice. I'm mired in shit so deep I don't know which way is up. Or out."

"It's easier dealing with someone else's problems, isn't it?"

"Seriously. I'd offer to trade, to fix yours and you fix mine, but I can't be trusted with that much responsibility." I laughed, but deep down, it scared me. What if I was in her situation with Dane?

I shivered. That was what would be worse than where I was now.

"I'm going to be honest, if it were me instead of you, I'd probably terminate."

"Really?" Lauren's eyes teared up. "Thank you so much for saying so. One of my friends got pregnant in high school and they shipped her off to a Swiss boarding school for 'young ladies in trouble.' Who the fuck calls it that anymore? And she didn't want to have the baby, but her parents made her and they adopted it."

"Oh my god. No. So much no. I mean, if that's what she wanted, fine. But otherwise, no."

"Would you tell Dane? Would you ask him to go with you?"

"Not only no, but hell no. But we're not close like you and Barclay are. You're best friends."

"Which is why I don't want to put this on his plate. I don't want him to think about it. I don't want him to hate me for what I'm going to do."

"So you do know what you're going to do?"

"I guess I do. I was afraid to say it."

I took her hand. "It's up to you whether you tell him or not, but I think if you don't, it's going to change your relationship anyway. It'll be a secret and you guys don't keep secrets from each other, do you?"

"No. We don't."

"Do you want me to go with you?"

"Would you?"

"Of course."

Lauren's eyes watered. "I don't know what I'd do without you."

I put my arm around her and held her close, much like what Shae had done for me the other night.

I hadn't had many female friends until now. I thought that all other girls were like Pandora or wanted to be Pandora.

But I needed friends. I needed these friends.

Without Dane, I never would've gotten close with them. I supposed I could thank him for that.

Someday, maybe I'd be able to thank him for doing what he

thought was right. Because honestly, how would I have pushed back against his father? Maybe I'd have found a way, but it would've made the road a lot harder.

Even without H2's interference, a future together was impossible. So it was best we severed whatever insanity that was and got on with our lives.

And maybe I should go to the game. Especially if he wasn't going to be there.

Of course, the idea of playing without him seemed wrong.

"Do you really think I should tell him?"

"I really do. He may have a lot of emotions about this, but in the end, I think he'll support what you want to do. It's the best option for you both."

"Can I tell you something?"

"Anything."

"Someday, I could see us doing this together. Barclay and I. Getting married. Having babies. The whole thing. But not yet. God, not yet."

"Maybe you should tell him that, too."

"We agreed if we weren't married by thirty-five, we'd say fuck it and do it. Have a few kids, buy a house with a yard and get a dog."

"And you keep telling me you're not in love. Okkkaaaay."

"We're not. We're not."

"Yeah."

"Really."

"Okay."

"We aren't."

"Are you trying to convince me or yourself?"

"Keep pushing and I'm going to drag you down to that game tonight."

"Since we're confessing, I'm really not up to it. The idea of anyone else's hands on me makes me want to cry."

"It didn't when we were playing at Bear Lake."

"Yeah, I know. And it's weird. I think I'd be into it if Hunt and I were still... doing whatever it was we were doing. I miss him so much. How dumb is that? Not too long ago, if you told me I'd never have to speak to him again, I'd have done anything to make that happen. Sacrifice a goat and dance naked across the football field during halftime? Got it. Suck twenty dicks? Done. Anything. Now, I wish I could rewind. I wish I could go back to Bear Lake." I avoided making eye contact with her. I was ashamed of my feelings. Huntington Dane III was an awful person.

I hated loving him.

But I did.

Maybe he even loved me back. That was the worst part of all this.

"Asher, you know he wouldn't have done what he did if he didn't care about you."

"I know. Double-edged sword, I guess."

"Sometimes, I think all feelings are. But then I remember that's nihilist bullshit and happiness is everywhere, if you just decide it is. There is no better feeling than loving someone else."

"Whelp, I think that settles it."

"What?" Lauren eyed me.

"If there is no better feeling than this, I should just go hang myself. Because this is the worst."

We laughed and laughed. We laughed so hard we cried. Even though it wasn't that funny.

She took a deep, shuddering breath. "Okay, no. Really. This part of it sucks, but this is one of the best parts about being human."

"You're probably right. I saw things in black and white before and having these feelings, everything is brighter. More colorful. Even the black cloud hanging over my head. It's more velvety."

We laughed some more.

"Okay, here's what we're going to do. We're going to call Shae. And she's going to tell us it's all going to be okay. Then we'll tell each other. It's going to work out."

"This is a good plan." I picked up my phone and dialed. "Hey," I said when she answered. "Come over. Bring ice cream. I have vodka."

"We're not crying again, are we? I don't want to cry tonight. I have a date," Shae said.

"Oh. Well. Let me hang up then. Because we're crying. But we decided we'd tell each other it's going to be okay."

"Who is we?"

"Oh, Lauren is here. Let me put you on speaker."

"I'll bring the ice cream. It is going to be okay, but only if there's no more crying. I can't have splotchy face," Shae said.

"Who are you going out with?" I asked.

"Justin... I forget his last name. He's cute. And he's not Bastian."

"Oh my god. Did Bastian ask you out?" Lauren squealed.

"Hell no. He asked me for sex. I told him I was busy and basically threw Justin under the bus."

"So wait, you don't want to have sex with Bastian?" I asked.

"I do. That's the problem. Everyone wants to have sex with Bastian and his ego would make it a threesome."

"That is pure truth right there," Lauren said. "But I've heard it's warranted. I mean, didn't your friend Jax opt for devirginization via Rathboner?"

"She did, but I don't know if that's happened yet or not. She's being close-lipped about it. Maybe because Matt is being weird," Shae replied. "What flavor ice cream?"

"That Halo Top stuff. We can eat a whole pint and it won't be too bad for the size of my thighs," Lauren said.

"Oh, that's a good one. I like those. The pistachio. Maybe the caramel macchiato. Or... or... the lemon cake. That one is good," I said.

"I'll just bring an assortment. See you soon." Shae hung up.

"Matt is so jealous of Bastian. I know he doesn't like Jax that way, he's just mad she didn't ask him," Lauren said.

"That's a weird thing to be jealous about. If he's not actually into her."

"Matt and Bastian have a rivalry that goes back to when they were kids."

"Huh. Kind of like me and Hunt."

"Yeah. Which was kind of why it was so hot to see Bastian give him that dance. Matt got all embarrassed but was trying really hard not to show it. I know it gave Bastian a thrill to have given him a boner."

"So much subtext."

"That's why we play. Drama." She shrugged.

"That's what Hunt said. He likes to play because he stirs the pot, so to speak. He said that's why people say they don't like to play with him, but they actually do." I flopped back on my bed. "Damn. Why can't I go for five minutes without talking about him?"

"It's okay. Talk about him. Then I don't have to think about my problem."

"We could both talk about Shae's problem... By the way, Barclay said he was going to talk to you about that."

"He hasn't. What did you have in mind?"

"Just a little matchmaking. If we don't get what we want right now, we can make sure she does."

"Hmm. Doesn't this make you guilty of doing the same thing to her that Hunt did to you?"

"No."

"Maybe."

"No." Was she right? "We're not taking away her choices. We're just putting her in situations to make her think about her choices differently."

"Uh huh."

"Barclay said you were really good at this kind of thing."

"Did he? Well, I do want her to be happy. Why do think she should be with Bastian?"

"Just a gut feeling I have."

Lauren grinned. "Yeah, me too. So you know the best way to make that happen right?"

"It is not Truth or Dare. She already has a date tonight anyway."

"Okay. We play other games on other nights. Sometimes, there's Seven in Heaven."

"She'd kill me."

"Oh wait... Never Have I Ever is a better one. Especially for those two." Lauren nodded.

I heard footsteps outside. I heard his voice. My first instinct was to run to the door and open it, but I held myself still. It was dumb, but I wanted just the sight of him. I needed to drink him in. I wanted to hear his voice.

Wear his t-shirt.

Lauren grabbed my hand and squeezed. "Just wait for the ice cream."

I nodded. Staring at him wasn't going to do me any good, but before I knew it, I was on my feet and drawn to the door.

Lauren flung herself against the door. "No."

"Yes."

"Nuh-uh."

I narrowed my eyes. "I want a water."

"Wait."

"No." Except she laughed.

Then I laughed, but I reached around her for the door and she blocked me.

"Don't make me—"

Except she tackled me mid-sentence. We crashed to the floor with a loud thump and she landed on top of me.

"Can you keep it down in there? Christ," Hunt growled through the door. "Some of us have to study."

"Some of us do, but you don't. So mind your business, Hunt," Lauren said through the door.

"I'm not in the mood for your shite, Lauren."

"You never are. Yet it's this awesome free service I provide."

The sound of his voice affected me in ways I didn't expect. No, maybe not unexpected. I knew it would make me sad, but it didn't know hearing his dry tones and sarcastic irritation would make me so happy.

My stupid eyes teared up.

I definitely didn't give them permission for that.

I opened the door. I ripped it open like ripping off a Band-Aid. To be honest, I was as startled as he was.

Face to face with him, I was overwhelmed with emotion. So many I couldn't parse them out. They all crashed over me at once.

"We're playing Truth or Dare. Wanna?"

He looked like I'd slapped him and I watched as he closed ranks. His eyes grew cold and chilly. His shoulders stiff and the expression on his face was one of pure arrogance.

"As if I'd play that game with you, Cinder Girl. You know how quickly I tire of my toys."

It would've been so easy to get angry with him for what he'd said.

So easy to fall into our old habits. Before Bear Lake. Before his father. I know it would've been easier for us both to pretend.

But fuck easy.

"Yeah, I do. But I also know you love me. You can deny it all you like. You can be as mean as you like. You can hate to love me. But you do." I poked his shoulder. "Love me."

"That's the most awful thing you've ever said to me Asher, I don't think I'll ever forgive you."

He retreated back to his room and for a moment, I was tempted to follow him. In the end, I didn't. I couldn't afford to lose my scholarship or my place at Hollingsworth.

That was when my phone rang.

I almost didn't answer it because I didn't recognize the number, but Lauren snatched it from me.

"You've reached National Necrophiliac's Society. You slay 'em, we lay 'em. How may I direct your call?"

And Lauren's face went white.

She held out the phone with shaking hands and hissed, "I am so fucking sorry. Oh my god, am I sorry."

I shrugged. "Whatever." I couldn't imagine anyone who'd be calling me this late that would make Lauren pale like that. Even my mother would've laughed at that.

"Hello?"

"Tuesday. After class. Report to the Miranda Hotel to begin your internship. Don't be late and don't wear knockoffs."

"Listen Pandora, you're not funny—

"Pandora Heyde? Not a chance. This isn't a joke. It's like you don't know who I am or that you applied for one of the most prestigious internships for women in business and got it."

Instead of saying that I hadn't applied, I asked, "Miranda Pollix?"

"Yes, you'll be Miranda's intern. And since I'm her personal assistant, you'll be my bitch. Now, do you need an advance on your paycheck for clothes?"

"Yes." I didn't hesitate.

"I'll have a card messengered over tomorrow. Be anything but late and poorly dressed. See you Tuesday."

The line went dead.

"Did that just happen?" I asked Lauren.

"I think it did."

"Holy shit."

"With her money and connections, Hunt's dad won't be able to touch you."

I looked at the door and considered what lay beyond it. "He did this for me. I'm sure that he did."

"I'm sure that he did, too."

"Why didn't he just say so?"

"I don't know. Maybe you should ask him?"

"Maybe I should. Or maybe you should call Barclay and get him to drag Hunt down to Truth or Dare."

"Or maybe you could lock yourselves in his room and make him play your game, by your rules."

A new sensation washed over me. One I'd been chasing, but wasn't quite sure I'd ever have. It was power. It was confidence.

It was hope.

"I've decided Huntington Dane III is going to be my first acquisition. Maybe it will all end it shit, but you know what? He defied his father for me. He saved me, but he made sure I could save myself. That's the kind of modern-day prince charming I'm looking for."

"Didn't you say you didn't need to be saved?"

"Maybe I did. Maybe he does, too."

"Well," Lauren began, "when the ice cream gets here, I will toast to Happily Ever After."

"May it always be a journey and not a destination."

Lauren saluted me and I began to plot.

DANE

MONDAY BROUGHT my father back to my doorstep and while it was
not unexpected, I was glad the pod was empty.

"Do you know what you've done?" he asked me, calmly.

"I do."

"Do you? How am I supposed to trust you?"

"You're not. Lesson one. Trust no one. That wasn't trust no one *but*
family. It was trust no one." I couldn't believe how calm I was.

"You did what I always knew you would. You let a piece of ass
break you."

My first instinct was to hit him, but he wanted to rile me. He
wanted a reaction. So I didn't give him one.

"If you say so."

"I'm going to end her, that girl."

"Are you? Probably not. She'll be interning for Miranda and under
her wing. She's safe."

"She will never be safe from me. Twenty years from now—"

"Oh, twenty years from now the board will have replaced you. With
me." I knew that was the future he both wanted and feared.

"I'm cutting you off."

"That's fine. I have my own money. There is literally nothing you can do to me."

"I can disown you." He didn't hesitate to play on the fear that he himself had instilled in me.

"That is also fine. Because you know what, you've never actually been a proper father to me. You can't take away what I never had. If you're finished..." I motioned to the door.

"You little bastard."

"No, that's Barclay, I'm afraid. Maybe he still has time for you. I, however, do not. Feel free not to call again. Love to the missus."

I closed the door and when I was sure he was gone, I let out a shaky breath. I was proud of myself, but it fucking hurt.

I had to accept I was never going to have the kind of father I wanted. I was never going to have his love or admiration. I had to live my life in such a way that it didn't matter to me.

He was going to go after anyone who got close to me, so I'd have to watch for that. If that meant being alone, I guess that's what it would mean.

My phone rang. It was my mum.

"Darling, are you okay?"

"I... yes."

"First, I'm proud of you for standing up to him. Second, was it really for the Warren girl?"

"It was for me." And for her.

"Oh. I've always like her. You know, it's not her fault that her father is a twatcrumpet."

Twatcrumpet? "Mum..."

"Is that not how you say it?"

"I have no actual idea what that is. Except that it's bad."

"It'll do well enough. I suppose he's threatened to disown you?"

"He did. I told him basically to get stuffed."

"Good. You should've rebelled a long time ago. It's what you're supposed to do."

"I didn't have anything to rebel against."

"And now you do? Come on, Hunt, tell me. It was for love, wasn't it?"

"Answer me something first. Did you love my father when you married him?"

She laughed. "Of course I thought I did. I was too innocent to know any better."

"Why stay?"

"I like my life. I'm comfortable. Why are you asking these things?"

"Because if love isn't real—"

"Oh, my little pie. Of course, it's real. Just because I didn't know the difference between infatuation and love doesn't mean it's not real. Don't you believe I love you?"

I suppose now that I thought about it, I *didn't* believe that she loved me. I thought of myself as the perfect accessory she'd made herself.

"Of course I know you love me."

"That's another reason I stayed. So you were given all the advantages that comes with being a Dane. So he could never usurp you, his firstborn."

"Well, he did. He disowned me. Like I said."

"Bah, he'll get over it. He'll be proud of you after he gets over his snit."

That was when I realized I finally didn't care. I knew it would come down to this. To finally getting the thing I craved most in the world when it didn't matter anymore.

"Neither of us want your life, Mum."

"No one does when they're young," she sighed wistfully.

"That's the problem. You start out thinking it's love, then you slide down into that pit of comfortable misery."

"Maybe it'll be different for you."

"It will be. Because we're not seeing each other."

"Don't you think maybe you should give it a chance before you throw it away? Let it grow to be what it was meant to be before you decide it's a thorn instead of a rose?"

"All roses have thorns."

"Like life. Ups and downs. You and Asher are right. You don't have to be us." She sighed. "You defied your father for her."

"Mum, it was for myself too. I couldn't live in his shadow forever."

"Of course not, but she was what made you stand up and say 'no more.' That's important. You should tell her so."

"No. She's pretty angry with me. Because I didn't stand up to him the first time."

"She'll forgive you. How could she not?"

"It's safer if she doesn't."

"Either you want to be us or you don't. I made the safe choice. I thought you didn't want that?"

I sighed. "Mum."

"What?"

"This is not a new button to push until you break it."

"Yes, it is. A new button, anyway. You've never shown any real interest in anyone. I don't want it to slip through your fingers. That's all. I just want you to be happy."

"I want that for you, too, Mum."

"I've made my choices and I'm happy enough. Who knows, maybe the stress of this will rupture something and he'll die." She coughed. "Sorry. He is your dad, so I shouldn't have said that. I do want you to have a good relationship with him."

"But you still want him to die so you can be the merry widow."

"The merriest."

"You could just divorce him."

"I could, but he wants me to. He's going to have to pull the pin on that one himself."

That was the dumbest place to draw the line in the sand. If neither of them was happy, why were they together? Neither needed the other. Or wanted the other. They both had affairs. I didn't understand it.

"You don't worry about your father and I, little love. Just be happy."

"What if being happy means dropping out of Hollingsworth and backpacking through Europe? Or just living on my trust?"

"Okay. I would hope you'd finish your education, but it's your life. It would also cause your father to jump up his own arsehole and pull it over his head like a cap. So, if you're feeling even more rebellious, you have my blessing."

This was not the answer I expected.

Yet, it was the one I needed.

I didn't want to drop out of university and go careening through the mountains on a yak, I just wanted to make my own choices and she seemed to understand that. Even if my father's discomfort and displeasure gave her obscene joy.

"I have to go, Mum."

"Bring her by for a visit. Or I'll come take her to tea at that Brit shop you like so much."

"Not yet. She still wants to set my face on fire."

"You'll smooth it over. She'll forgive you because you're you. My amazing and wonderful son."

"Actually, I don't know if you remember that John Warren wanted to formally introduce us when we were young and she said no because I was the bane of her existence."

"Did she actually tell you that?" My mother laughed and laughed. "Oh, it's meant to be. I remember how you went on about that girl."

"I did not."

"Yes, you did. Anyway, hang up with me and call her."

And my mother hung up.

The adult thing to do would be to talk to Asher, but in person. Not on the phone. To explain. If she'd listen to me.

The idea of this was almost as terrifying as confronting my father. I had no idea how to talk to her. Or if I even should.

I supposed that the *should* part would work itself out.

This still made my skin itch like it was too tight.

But like I said. I didn't want to be my father.

She'd asked me if I wanted to play Truth or Dare again, and maybe we should because that's when everything changed.

Maybe it could help me change it again. Not back to what it was, because that was over and I was okay with that.

It was new, unsure and untested, and we'd been tested now. Broken.

This new incarnation would be more durable. Something solid. It surprised me how much I wanted it.

I wanted all of Asher.

Not just her ass in her footie jams.

And I didn't want to be a danger to her or her future.

I'd told her I wasn't going to warn her away from me. I'd told her I was the villain, but that's not who I was and not who I wanted to be.

I wondered if that was going to be enough.

If I was going to be enough.

I was trying to plan my grand gesture when I heard her come in the pod and it sounded like she was crying.

I gave her a few minutes before I knocked on her door.

"No."

She was definitely crying. I could hear it in her voice.

"What's wrong, Cinder Girl? Did you lose your second-hand clog?" When she didn't respond again, I said, "Come on, love. I'll buy you another."

When it became apparent my teasing wasn't having the desired effect, I said, "Let me in, Asher."

I'd never heard her cry before, much less seen it. Oh, I'd seen tears gather in her eyes, but it was usually because she was enraged. She was one of those who once the tears started, it was time to duck and cover because murder was imminent.

Something had hurt her, cut her deep.

Whatever that something was, I was prepared to hunt it down and present it to her in tribute.

"The door is open," she murmured.

She looked so small, so broken, her arms wrapped around her knees while she sat on the floor. Her eyes were red and swollen. Just seeing her like this took the bricks that made up the foundation of what I believed about the world and shattered them. Turned them to dust.

"I can't fight with you now."

I sat down next to her and pulled her into my arms. She came easily, melted against me. She was all pliant and soft, and I handled her like I would a baby bird with a broken wing.

Gently. Carefully. Mindful of her broken places.

I stroked her back and allowed her to wrap around me. I'd never felt more privileged that she trusted me in this moment. Even after what had happened with my father.

She shuddered and sobbed.

I wanted to ask her what was wrong. How to fix it. How to make her stop making that sound because it cut through me like a dull blade, tearing as it went.

But I just held her and waited.

Finally, she sniffled. "I'm sorry."

"Don't be sorry, Cinder Girl. Just tell me how to fix it, and I swear to you, I will."

She pulled back and looked up into my eyes, as if she were searching for something there. I don't know what she saw, but she nodded slowly. "I believe you would, if you could, but no one can fix this."

"Then tell me what you need."

She wrapped around me again, more tightly this time. As if she were afraid I was going to disappear. "This. I need this."

I stroked her hair, her back, and kissed the top of her head until she stilled again.

"I hated him, you know."

"Who did you hate?"

"My father. I hated him so much for what he did, but he didn't do what we all thought. He wasn't..." She sniffed. "He was a criminal shit. I can say that. He was. Except he didn't leave us high and dry with his secretary."

"What happened?"

"They found his body today on Grand Cayman. She was with him. They'd been killed by the cartel he was laundering money for. He's been dead all this time." She exhaled a shudder. "I feel so stupid for crying about it now. I cried when he left, and I hated him for a long time. Hating him or not doesn't make him any less dead."

I tried to imagine what it would be like to be in her position. If it were my father, but I couldn't.

"It's okay to cry."

"Would you?"

"Well, no. I'm a Dane. I don't have feelings, remember?" I teased her.

"Fucker." But she didn't make any move to get away from me.

"It'll be okay, you know."

"I know. Because we'll make it okay for ourselves."

"We will." I wanted to tell her I'd gone a long way to doing just that, but I knew this wasn't the time. As much I wanted it to be.

"Thank you," she whispered.

"For what?" Okay, maybe it was the time. She opened the door and while I may not be a shite anymore, I was still an opportunist. I was going to make her say it.

"For this." She sighed again. "For the paid internship with a patron who will help me live to be a big fish."

"Did she tell you it was me?"

"Of course, she did. After her assistant called me, the lady herself did, too. She told me all about your little talk."

"You still hate me?"

"Hate to love you," she whispered.

I realized then she didn't need any kind of grand gesture. She just needed what she'd told me all along.

Just me.

It was a pretty fucking novel of a concept to me.

"Hate to love you, too." I kissed the top of her head again.

"Listen. We're going to date, okay? I don't want any argument. I don't want to hear any crap about our parents. We won't be them. We'll be us. The mistakes we make, our wins, our losses, that's all us," Asher demanded.

"What if we can't help but become them?"

"Free will. We choose every step of the way. I'm done with fear. I'm done with what if. I want right now. And I want you. And guess what else?"

"What?" I found myself aroused by her demands. I liked it when she told me how things were going to be.

"You are going to give me everything I want."

If anyone else had said that to me, I'd have thought they were only after my money. My position. My family name.

But not Asher. She wanted something money couldn't buy, and that made me want to give her everything it could.

"I said I wasn't going to warn you away from me, Cinder Girl, because I'm the villain."

"You did, but I think we both know that's bullshit."

"I need you to be safe, Asher. I need to know that I'm not toxic for you or the life you want." I inhaled the scent of her. "Your dreams. Because our parents had dreams once too."

"They did and they made their choices. I was going to say that I guess if you really don't want me...offer you a way out, but you know what? No. You said you love me. You're mine. That's it. No take backs. You're my boyfriend now. Suck it up, Prince Smarming. Your princess is in *this* castle."

"What happened to being the dragon?"

"We'll take turns. Today I'm the princess. Maybe I'll be the dragon tomorrow. Maybe we'll both be dragons tomorrow. I don't care. As long as we're together."

"As you wish."

And I kissed her for all I was worth.

ASHER

WHEN THE SHIT hit the fan, I never expected it would be Huntington Dane that I wanted.

The one I needed.

But he was.

It was like I'd shattered into a hundred thousand tiny shards and just the sound of his voice had started to put me back together. His arms were strong enough to hold me while I made myself whole again.

If you'd told me a month ago, he'd be the one I needed, I'd have laughed in your face. Let's be honest, I probably would've lit you on fire.

Yet here I was.

Here *we* were.

Nothing had ever been more right.

His kiss was so much more than a kiss. It was a promise for the future and a declaration of right now.

It lit me on fire in ways I never knew I needed to burn.

A friend once told me she loved her boyfriend because their broken pieces fit together like a puzzle. I'd always thought that was beautiful, and I thought I'd wanted that for myself.

Being with Hunt wasn't like that at all. We didn't fit together until we made ourselves whole on our own, and that was beautiful too. That was better for me, and for Hunt.

The best thing about this was that I wasn't afraid anymore. I'd spent so long being afraid of the future, of myself, of making the wrong choices. Of being trapped into the same circle I'd been in my whole life.

This news about my dad had flayed me open, but it also turned on a light and I still had a lot of baggage to go through, but it was all going to be okay.

Because I had myself.

And I had Hunt.

Man, did I have him.

When I pulled off his shirt, I thought about how I had his broad shoulders, his strong biceps, and his hot, hot mouth.

God, again, I wondered how I'd ever thought he was cold.

Once upon a time, I'd imagined he'd be icy to the touch, but it was all fire and lightning. Everywhere he touched me was alive in a way I'd never felt before, but needed more of.

"Is it shitty of me to be getting in your knickers while you're grieving?" He whispered in my ear.

"Grief sex is life-affirming," I said back.

"Good. Because we're going to have grief sex, then I'm going to fuck you through the wall and then—" he pressed his hot mouth against my throat.

"And then?"

"Then I'm going to make love to you."

"Mmm." I arched to give him better access. "You're not going to make hate to me? You're not going to make me cum in retaliation for turning you on?"

"Maybe after I show you how much I love you."

"Good. Because I want all of you, Hunt. No walls between us. Only truth."

He stopped and looked into my eyes. Our breath mingled and I wanted him to kiss me again, but I wanted this too. This truth. This moment that hung gravid with so much possibility.

"Only truth? The truth is, I'm terrified of this. Of you."

I pressed my palm against his cheek and his eyes flashed dark.

"But I'd do anything to keep it. I'm afraid of being weak. I'm afraid of losing you. I'm afraid of hurting you. I'm afraid of hurting myself, too."

"I think love is just like that."

"I understand why people don't want it. I didn't want it."

"I know. So tell me again."

"I love you, Cinder Girl."

I kissed him again, wanting to taste those words on his lips while they echoed inside me. I wanted to hold them tight even as the breath they were whispered on was carried away.

"Nuh-uh," he said against my lips. "Your turn."

I laughed. "For what?"

"Come on, tell me. This is a partnership, right? Step up."

I laughed again. I liked knowing that he needed and wanted to hear me say it as much as I did. "I love you."

He pushed me down on the floor and somehow I was naked. He'd managed to undress me while he was still mostly dressed.

"That's not fair," I said, and reached for his belt.

"No one said this was going to be fair." He captured my hands and pushed them above my head while he dipped his mouth to my breast. "Be a good girl and hold them there until I'm done."

"No way. Like I'm just some object for you to have your way with?"

"Not some object. The woman I want to worship with my mouth."

Well, I wasn't going to argue with that.

"Fine. This time, I'll let you worship me. But just this time."

"Shh," he whispered and kissed me. "Unless you're telling me how better to pleasure you, be quiet and let me."

"Yes, sir."

"Oh, or that. I could get used to that."

"Don't bother, it's not going to happen again."

"We'll see about that."

The smug look on his face gave me a flash of delicious fear. I'd wondered what it was like to be the center of his attention and I was about to find out.

He played my body like an instrument of which he was a master. He knew exactly where and how to touch me. I'd never been so high.

At least, not since the last time we'd done this.

Yet, it got better.

His mouth was a weapon, so were his hands, and this had become an all-out war. One I was fine with losing. I'd already surrendered anyway.

When he finally dipped his head between my thighs, I was begging him both to stop and to give me more. I'd never wanted to move my hands more. To push them through his hair, to dig my nails into his back, to touch him everywhere the way he'd touched me.

But I kept them above my head, as he instructed.

Even when I was digging my nails into my palms and screaming like he was murdering me.

As the hurricane of sensation passed over me, I was in his arms again and I struggled to catch my breath, to find the ground. I was flying and didn't know how to land.

And this fucker was still wearing pants.

I narrowed my eyes.

"Don't worry, Cinder Girl. I'm not done yet. Not by a long shot."

"You know, if you actually kill me..."

"Are you done already?" he teased.

I realized it would always be like this. All the best things would be a competition that we'd help each other win.

"Not a chance." I pounced and pushed him over onto his back. "My turn."

He laughed, but when he put his hands at my hips, I grabbed them and pushed them above his head.

"Nuh-uh. Same rules apply, Prince Smarming."

"Okay, do your worst, Cinder Girl."

"Nope. I'm going to do my very best."

He smiled at me and said, "I dare you."

And I did.

Then he did again.

And I... you get the picture?

I don't know what's going to happen, what the future is going to bring, but I know I want to face it with my Prince Charming.

Because the truth is, we're going to dare to be happy.

SPIN THE BOTTLE

The fun and games continue at Ridgemont Hall with Spin the Bottle. Keep with the RH gang by signing up for my newsletter here: www.sarawylde.com

Spin the Bottle
  Fast Times at Ridgemont Hall #2

Jax

I'm a virgin, but I don't want to be. I just want to get it over with, so I made a list. I held interviews. (I know, I'm a total Type A.) The winner is Sebastian Rathbone. Grade A Beefcake who plays defense for the Grizzlies' Rugby team. Manwhore extraordinaire. So basically, a professional. The problem? My best friend, Matt. For some reason, he wanted me to pick him. I'd never choose him because then I'd fall in love and I remember the hell that was middle school. Now that he's grown into his head and feet, and he is by definition also Grade A Beefcake, there's even less chance he'd ever feel more than friendship for me. Why put myself through that? I thought I'd locked all of that away until a game of Spin the Bottle makes me doubt everything. Especially the lie I've been telling myself about not being in love with my best friend.

Matt

Sebastian Rathbone? Dude. No way. He's not a bad guy, but he's not the guy for Jax. If anyone knows the guy for Jax, that's me. It hurts I wasn't even consulted. Actually, what bothers me the most is that she didn't ask me to be the one. To punch her V-Card, I mean. I'm pretty good at what I do, or so I've been told. It should be a good memory. Something special. And lemme tell you, Rathboner isn't going to make it special for anyone. I don't like it that there's this part of her she's going to give to someone else, but I guess I have to get right with it. I'm the best friend. Not the lover. Except when faced with losing her, I'll have to take a spin on chance just one more time.

Out September 18!

www.ingramcontent.com/pod-product-compliance
Lightning Source LLC
Chambersburg PA
CBHW071718140626
46557CB00012B/955